Tiers of the Imperiums™

Wilting Souls

Book 1 of the
Wilting Souls Saga

CRJ Riggins

Author's note

HUMANITY GRINDS EVERY PIECE OF happiness and joy out of life. Then when a person fades into darkness, humanity begs them to be humane.

In which that person can proudly reply...
"I am."

~ CRJ Riggins ~

I drew influence from many cultures and
civilizations around the world when I wrote this story. Feel free to
check out the meaning
behind the names used for characters, empires, planets, and
terminologies.

Prologue

Imperial Date: 2141 ABCAE
Adrasteia binary cycles after establishment
Month, day: Thoth, 15th

Location: Planet Adrasteia

Reign: Emperor Quortez and Empress Felicia
Population: Fifty-one point one billion

THE WIND HAD PICKED UP, whipping Takumbo's dreadlocks into her face as she watched Lord General Bandares form a voidship out of the nano-material flowing freely throughout the raging river beneath his feet.

"I'll never see you again will I?" Takumbo thought to herself as she shifted her gaze from Bandares, to the people standing around her.

Seeing their solemn faces only caused her further grief, and she couldn't help but wonder what made a person's fate so utterly unavoidable. Placing her hand on her stomach, Takumbo sent best wishes to the tiny fetus growing within her.

"I'll do my best to protect you and your half brothers and sisters. And I'll even fight fate itself if it's as cruel as the one I feel awaits your father."

Bringing her gaze back to Bandares, Takumbo could see the nano-material completely covering all but his emotionless face. Inhaling deeply, holding tears locked firmly in her eyes, she sent him a mental farewell. Moments later, just before the black orb of nano-material rose into the void, Takumbo felt the presence of Bandares touch her mind.

"Takumbo, I entrust with you all of my adult memories. Learn from them. Teach the children that the small choices they make, have the potential to make a very large impact. Most importantly, teach them to hold steadfast when outside forces try to destroy the kindness inside them."

"Bandares, I believe you're still a kind man, no matter what you've done in the past. I wish you could see what I see inside of you," she replied telepathically, feeling Bandares withdraw his presence from her mind - only leaving behind a beautiful sacred geometric pattern which contained his memories.

"What could you have done that'd make you feel so guilty, you'd run away from teaching these lessons yourself?" She wondered, feeling tears finally escape her eyes.

Fighting them back, Takumbo pressed her mind into the sacred geometric pattern, curious what could lead a man to hate himself to such a degree. Quickly adjusting her mind to the complicated pattern, she began to see snips and pieces of Bandares's memory play out.

"I don't think I can do this!" She thought as her body began to involuntarily tremble from the little she'd already saw and felt.

"Sit and close your eyes; we'll stay and help," a melodic voice said from behind.

Before she could comply, Takumbo felt and heard the woman's voice travel inside her. As the woman continued to sing, Bandares's memories unfolded into a blurry mirage of image and sound with no beginning or end.

"I'll be your anchor," Takumbo heard another woman say inside her mind, feeling the woman's presence taking hold of her unsteady thoughts.

A few moments later, Takumbo saw the sacred geometric pattern dissolve completely. In its place stood the figure of Banderas in his earlier cycles of life.

"Very few people are like you Takumbo. You have rekindled something in me I thought I'd lost. The person I am today and the cruel, cold-blooded person I'm known to be throughout the Empire, was not always so. Thank you for holding a mirror in front of me. Until you, I truly thought I'd lost the ability of self-reflection. Come, bear witness to the events that lead to the wilting of my soul."

When the young Bandares finished speaking, Takumbo felt herself pulled inside him. In that moment, she almost felt as if they were one and the same person.

"We'll start here," Banderas said, sounding as if it were her own thought.

Through his eyes, she could see him staring at a real time hologram of the R'yu solar system. In front of him, young men were wrestling and jesting about, with the overall mood of the chamber appearing to be happy and calm.

"I finally asked a question I don't want to know the answer to," she realised, hearing a man scream as blood gushed out of his mouth...

Chapter I

Hopeless

Four hundred sixty-five cycles ago

Imperial Date: 1676 ABCAE

Location: Adrasteia controlled, R'yu solar system, planet R'yu

Reign: Empress Dakini, "The Blood Empress"
Population: Fifty billion of which thirty billion are slaves

BANDARES WAS WATCHING THE ASTEROIDS of the shattered planets enter the atmosphere of R'yu on his holographic-imager when he heard Nepson scream. Without a second thought, he grabbed his medical pack and rushed to him. By the time he reached him, Nepson had begun violently convulsing. Panicking, Bandares opened the medical pack and nervously took out an anti-vector infuser, then slowly pressed it to Nepson's neck.

"What are you doing?" Squad leader T'mot bellowed from halfway across the chamber.

"I'm trying to save his life!" Bandares retorted, upping the dose of pathogen inhibitors in anticipation for what the newly appointed Squad leader was going to say.

"Get that thing off him, let him die. We're becoming full citizens tomorrow, so let's cut the mushy teamwork crap out. It's back to the way it should be, every man for himself. And he'll be one less man for any of us to worry about."

The cold words made Bandares blind with anger.

"You must be the stupidest squad leader in the history of the Empire to say that. And seriously! How can all of you just stand there, going along with him? Wouldn't you want someone to save you?" He screamed, fixing the people nearest to him with accusing looks before finally resting his gaze back on T'mot.

"What'd you say?" I want to record it so I can lay it in one of your statued hands after I beat you to death," T'mot replied, giving Bandares a dark look that let him know he was completely serious about his claim.

"You heard what I said T'mot. Don't think you're so high and mighty. You got squad leader by fluke accident yesterday; and you're right, today is our last day here. Meaning, I don't give a damn about anything you have to say, you selfish asteroid dwelling scum," he replied, feeling Nepson's convulsions stop.

"By Yoginis grace," he muttered, realising why Nepson had stopped convulsing.

"Looks like you wasted your precious meds on a dead thing. If you grew up in the shattered debris like most R'yu people, you'd know good resources are hard to come by and that you should keep them for yourself. Who are you going to save if you can't even save yourself?

You just pumped all your meds into the dead thing right there, and I'm not giving you an ounce of mine. Besides, I'm not dumb enough to ignore brain worm symptoms like the dead thing you're holding. Idiots deserve to die; that's what natural selection is for."

Every time T'mot called Nepson a thing instead of a person, Bandares felt his eyes twitch. Looking down, he could already see the eggs of the brain worm slithering down Nepson's nose, causing him to shutter in disgust.

"HEY!" Bandares heard before seeing a bright burst of speckles as T'mot's foot connected with the side of his head.

The force of the kick was so violent he couldn't feel the pain or hear anything in his left ear as he collapsed. Only cycles of arduous training kept him from blacking out, but it wasn't enough to help him regain any sort of motor function to protect himself from the kicks that followed to his body and face.

"Don't...You...Ever...Look...Away!" Bandares finally made out, as he rolled across the ground from T'mot's final kick.

How could these people be so selfish, even after all the training we've gone through? Don't they see we need to stick together no matter what? He thought as he tried to implement the mental technique the Yoginis priestess had begun to teach them, whereby a person could turn pain into pleasure.

What am I missing from the technique? Everything still hurts, he thought weakly as he tried to make himself stand.

"You should stay on the ground and keep the dead thing company," T'mot said snidely.

"Enough is enough!" Bandares wheezed out, feeling pieces of his rib snap and protrude into his lung.

"Every time I'm nice, I get hurt," he reflected gaining his resolve.

"I'm tired of you...just plain sick and tired of your crap," he grunted, feeling the pain in his chest subside as rage overtook him.

Pushing himself off the ground, Bandares charged towards T'mot. As his feet moved faster, everything in the surrounding area appeared to move slower, until finally time itself seemed to be at a standstill. Reaching T'mot, he took a short powerful jab with his right, aiming directly for his navel. Then followed up with a spinning uppercut to T'mot's chin with his left. The sound and the feeling of T'mot's jaw and teeth fracturing under his knuckles instantly made him cringe, causing him not to follow through with another attack.

"Maybe he'll leave me alone now," he hoped optimistically, watching T'mot fall backwards in slow motion.

Somewhere during his mid fall, time seemed to flow normally again, and by the time he heard T'mot hit the ground, he'd already turned to retrieve his medical pack.

"Raa!" He heard just as he knelt in front of the pack.

Without looking, he kicked backward and felt his barefoot connect with T'mot's stomach.

"Why are you still trying? How are you still trying? Give it up! You lost!" He choked out as blood from his punctured lung hit his vocal chords.

"Where's the healing gel? How'd it suddenly disappeared?" He thought frantically, feeling his lung rapidly growing heavier.

"All right! I yield, I yield!" He heard T'mot gurgle.

In that very same moment, Bandares felt something hard and blunt smash across his head, and before he knew it, he lay sprawled out on his back, looking up at the bloody ruin of T'mot's face.

"Rule number one, never trust your enemy. Lying to deceive the enemy is of the utmost honor," T'mot said just before spitting blood and broken chunks of teeth into his face.

"Or have you forgotten how us so called asteroid dwelling scum have survived for hundreds of thousands of cycles. Oh wait, I almost forgot you're a weak planet born kunuss. I don't know how I almost missed the smell! You must've taken a long bath today!"

"No, T'mot it's all the blood from your broken face. That's why you can't smell. Come...come a little closer," he replied, ready to put T'mot to sleep with his next attack.

"Mmm, no that's alright, I can smell you from here. But I'm thinking of changing your scent from foul kunuss to rotting corpse.

Yhea, yhea that's right, I'll give you the same fate I gave our late squad leader U'te'el!" T'mot snarled as he raised his booted foot over his head.

Bandares felt any remaining strength left in him drain out after hearing the truth behind U'te'el's demise.

"Hopefully in the next life, a team will mean just that," he thought closing his eyes.

"It's almost time for all of you to receive the title of citizen, from that of slave. Life will become much harder for all of you and death much easier. I wonder if there are any among you worthy enough to enter my kunuss and possibly give me a child," a soft female voice said cutting through the almost silent chamber, causing Bandares's stilled heart to race once more.

With every ounce of strength he had left in his body, he rolled onto his stomach, placed his hands over his forehead and said.

"For her honor, I live! For her honor, I die! For her honor, I give my seed! For her honor, I give her my all!"

Shuttering from the pain, Bandares's only concern was that his praise be in perfect unison with all the others. Beside him, he could hear T'mot breathing wetly and wondered how bad it must've hurt him to move his mouth in its current state.

"All may rise, unless you cannot, then you may lay," the woman said nonchalantly, making Bandares want to stand that much more.

"Who is she? I don't recognise her voice or her scent. She smells like she just came off a voidship," he thought, inching his torso back in a feeble attempt to kneel before her.

"You look like a fine specimen. My implants tell me your name is T'mot. I want your seed inside me," he heard the woman say, now sounding mere inches away from him.

"Pain is pleasure," he kept thinking over and over, forcing himself up to a kneeling position, just in time to see an almost completely nude ebony-skinned woman reach out and take T'mot's hand.

"All of you go back to what you were doing, unless you plan to watch us. That's totally fine by me. But don't watch too long; my advice is to sleep as much as you can. Tomorrow will be the longest day of your lives. Or the shortest, depending on who you are," the woman said, fixing Bandares with a gaze that chilled his spine.

T'mot had seen the way the woman regarded him, then shot him a disgusting, slack jaw, no-teeth smile that made Bandares wish he'd broken his eye sockets along with his jaw.

"I'll kill you for what you did to U'te'el, and for what you've done to me," he

promised himself, watching T'mot turn to follow the woman as she walked towards one of the nearest beds.

Many of the men who had stood silent while watching the fight between T'mot and himself, quickly surrounded the bed. Short moments later, he could hear the sounds of love making, which was quickly drowned out by loud cheers of excitement and encouragement.

"I'm going to drown in my own blood while everyone ignores me. No one here values another person's life when its right in front of them, yet all seem happy about the act of creating a new one. How come people's actions never make any sense to me? Would T'mot or the others want their child to suffer and die like this? If I survive, I don't ever want to become like them," he thought, swaying dizzily on his knees.

"I think you're looking for this," he heard from his left.

As he turned his head, a syringe containing the healing gel he'd been looking for hit his nose, bounced off, and then hit the floor in front of his knees. Snatching it up quickly, he undid the sanitary cap, jammed the needle into his lung and pressed the button.

"AH!" Bandares screamed as the gel interacted with his internal wounds.

The pain was nothing like he'd ever felt before, and he couldn't tell if it felt like fire or ice consuming his lung.

"I wasn't going to give it back to you, you know? I figured you were going to die anyway, so why should I. Anyways, don't prove me right or I'll be mad I wasted it on you," the man said, sounding closer than before.

"Yon'tu? Why? Our whole time here, we've shared everything. Why would you take the gel when I needed it the most?"

"You shared with me, I never shared with you. You were the only one who ever truly shared anything with anyone. And I guess you were so delusional, you took our happiness at your stupidity as us sharing back with you. But I think deep down inside, you knew the truth, which is why you probably fought even harder to believe your own stupidity. You wanted to tell yourself that you weren't falling victim to your kindness, to self-validate your actions. But you knew, yhea I'm definitely certain you knew."

"I," Bandares began, but Yon'tu cut him off.

"Since I do feel a bit guilty taking advantage of your...I can't think of a better word, other than stupidity. I'll give you some advice, never let people take advantage of you, especially your kindness. And when you know someone is doing so, never make excuses for why that person is mistreating you."

Yon'tu sucked his teeth, shaking his head in disappointment, then said, "You better not die anytime soon. I feel wasting words on dead things is worse than anything else."

Bandares felt the harsh truth of Yon'tu's words eat into him, overtaking the pain he felt in his body. Standing up and facing Yon'tu, he took in the details of his passive, nonchalant face, then turned and hobbled to his bed. Falling into it, he closed his eyes and forced himself to sleep.

"Cum, cum deep inside me. Yes, cum in my kunuss," Bandares heard a woman moan.

Opening his eyes, the first thing he noticed was that his chamber was in night cycle.

"Still hurts," he mumbled rolling over onto his right to find the man who occupied the bed next to his, deep in the thralls of love making with a thick and beautiful ivory-skinned woman, who just so happened to be facing him.

"Cum for me O'ron" she whispered again, looking deep into Bandares's eyes before smiling and biting her bottom lip.

"I'm cuming! Ah I'm cuming!" O'ron bellowed seconds later.

What in the seven lives is going on? He thought breaking eye contact with the woman as she teasingly began to lick her lips.

And it's not just them, he realised fully awakening to the sounds and scents of his barrack's chamber.

Sitting up quickly, he saw exactly what his senses had alerted him to.

"Wow," he whispered, seeing every man in the barrack's chamber just as equally enthralled as O'ron.

From what he could see, only beds belonging to the dead and Yon'tu were unoccupied.

Is this part of the citizenship ceremony? Why does everyone else get to lose their virginity to such beautiful women? Why am I being left out? Is it because I was injured? Maybe there's a woman still here waiting for me to wake up. And where's Yon'tu? Maybe he is with a woman on the floor," he thought frantically, succumbing to intense jealousy.

Hopping out of his bed, he scanned the long barrack's chamber looking for any signs of a solo woman or to see if his presumption about Yon'tu's location was correct.

"This can't be right!" He whispered over and over, taking a few steps away from his bed in order to peer around some of the pillars obstructing his view.

After quickly searching the areas that had been blocked before, he was still unable locate Yon'tu or any unaccompanied woman within the chamber.

"AH! I hate this!" He grumbled as his jealousy gave birth to new feelings of sadness and longing.

Shakily, he walked through the center of the chamber, feeling his kudock growing harder with each passing step thinking, *this is unbearable, I wish I could get out of here!*

Opting to look away from the people making love, he focused his attention down the length of the chamber towards the thick round blast door that served as the chamber's only entrance and exit.

"It's unlocked!" He realised the moment his eyes took in the soft blue indicator lights embedded inside the door.

Quickening his paces to a near run, he made it to the door, then pressed his hand against it. With incredible speed the door rolled open sending a burst of hot, humid air rushing into his face.

"Am I allowed out or is this open for the women? Wait, what am I thinking? Women have the clearance to come and go as they please. But if the door is open, doesn't that mean I have the clearance as well?" He thought nervously stepping past the threshold of the open door, out into the honeycomb shaped passageway.

Holding his breath, looking both ways, he expected reprimand to come from someone at any moment. When nothing happened, he exhaled gratefully, then decided he would go left, towards the Blood Goddesses Temple. Thinking that if anyone caught him, he would say he assumed the door was left open for those wishing to go pray before inauguration as a citizen.

"Even though I know my plan sounds ridiculous, I need to get away from there. But am I risking everything? I only need to wait two more hours before the ceremony is supposed to begin," he considered as he requested his implants to display current time.

"What if my punishment for doing this is a life sentence as a slave?" Jumped in his mind, nearly stopping him in his tracks.

"They're energetic this year, are they not?" Bandares heard a woman's voice say further down the passageway.

"They are indeed. How many did you have so far?" Another woman replied.

"Crap, they're heading this way, what do I do? Should I stick with my stupid plan?"

Right after the thought crossed his mind, two nude, very thick and well-rounded women appeared from behind a slight curve in the passageway, directly in his line of sight.

"It's too late to run!" He realised, feeling his heart leap into his throat as the small amount courage he'd mustered from safely making out the door bled out.

"With honor, I serve her! With honor, I serve my all! Please forgive my trespasses," he proclaimed, throwing himself to the floor, palms up and head down.

"I've had four so far. It'll be interesting to see whose seed wins. Two cycles ago, I was surprised it wasn't any of the men I thought it'd be," Bandares heard the woman reply.

"My life," he started to say.

"Oh, really. I've only had three. The last one kept me for way too long, but honestly he was fun and full of energy. Look, some of his cum is still on my face. Taste it; I think he's quite fertile," Bandares heard the other woman reply.

Curious as to why he was being ignored, Bandares tilted his head to the left just in time to see both women's legs rising as they literally stepped over him. The utter disregard of his presence only strengthened his fear. In his mind, the women were regarding him as if he were already dead, with no need to expend energy reprimanding him.

"I serve all women gratefully! I await instructions!" He blurted, turning his body around to face the direction in which the woman were walking, while still maintaining his submissive position.

"Huh?" One of the woman asked almost under her breath sounding confused, sending fresh waves of panic coursing through him.

Taking a shallow breath, Bandares began to repeat himself, but before he spoke, he heard the two women start to whisper.

"What are they deciding?" He wondered, nervously biting his bottom lip.

"Rise," one of the women commanded.

Bandares shot up as quickly as he could, then bowed deeply, somehow reawaking the pain in his chest that'd been slowly ebbing away since he'd gotten out of bed.

"Thank you, with my life I…,"

"Your honor is noted; we require nothing at this moment. Where are you heading at this hour Tier one Bandares?" The heavier and shorter of the two women asked, sounding only mildly curious.

"I am heading to the temple to pray for strength so that I may serve all women as the Blood Goddesses wish all men to do," Bandares said proudly, feeling his knees knocking at the sound of his own voice telling his freshly concocted story.

Even through the fear, his mind raced at the implications of the way he'd just been addressed, thinking.

"Tier one Bandares? Does this mean I'm already considered a citizen? With no ceremony or any type of formality? Unless losing one's virginity is the ceremony. I shouldn't have left! Maybe one of them were on their way to visit me. Should I go back there and wait?"

"Ah… makes sense. How honorable you are. We would save you the trip and be your vessels for prayer, but unfortunately neither of us are on our cycle. Don't let us stop you. Carry on Tier one Bandares. May the sixty four Yoginis spirits guide you, and may the blood the Yoginis priestess share with you, give you strength in your conviction."

Bandares was now sweating so profusely he could smell, as well as feel the droplets running down his armpits and the back of his thighs.

"At your word, it becomes my bond," Bandares said breathlessly, tilting his head up while still maintaining his bow so the women could look into his eyes and see he meant no deception.

Neither woman held their gaze and the look they both wore before turning away seemed as if they'd just heard something mildly funny. Before he could muster up the courage to ask why he'd been regarded as Tier one instead of servant, they'd completely turned around and had already started to walk away, picking up their conversation as if nothing had ever happened.

"Damn it! I can't go back that way. I gave them my word," he thought solemnly, turning and walking toward the temple.

Within five minutes, he arrived in front of the temple and found himself truly wanting to go in for the first time in his life, hoping that this time he'd receive some form of spiritual guidance. Walking past the oils, candles and incense, he took in the details of the sixty-four Yogini statues in various forms of love-making, and felt a pang of jealousy return as he recalled what was happening in his barrack's chamber.

"The women were speaking of men from the other chambers – so maybe Yon'tu was taken to one of the other chambers," he thought, feeling hopeless as he walked up to the Blood Goddess statue of Kali standing atop a headless man.

Taking in the details of her trident and sword in her two right hands, with the head of the decapitated man oozing blood into a golden bowl in her two left hands, he couldn't help but empathize with the man.

"From your mercy, I still live. From your mercy, I am allowed to die in the service of your daughters," Bandares mumbled robotically as he turned to his right and regarded the dark red statue of the Blood Goddess's daughter, Vajrayogini.

"Vajrayogini, from your bloody womb I came into being. From your blood-filled womb, you nourished me. And through your daughters' bloody wombs, I pay homage to thee," he said enduringly, feeling more connection with Vajrayogini than with her blood thirsty and cold-blooded mother Kali.

Moving his fingers to the statue, he ran his fingers over the kunuss and nipples that dripped with a red, mineral substance that resembled blood.

"Do you not have other duties beside this?" Bandares heard a Yogini priestess ask from inside the temple.

Looking up from his finger, Bandares wondered who the priestess was speaking to, slightly hoping it was Yon'tu so that he wouldn't feel so alienated and alone. Inching forward, hoping to eavesdrop without being seen, he finally caught a whiff of air coming from inside the temple, making him both aroused and somewhat sick as the blend of sixty-four female cycles filled his nostrils.

"Sex is not a duty we're bound to priestess. Cleaning the deceased and petrifying them is," Bandares heard a woman reply, in a warm sultry voice.

"Sex is not, but bearing children is. Why miss this opportunity to try?" Bandares heard another Yogini priestess say.

Inching closer, resting on a thick pillar between the inside and outside of the temple, Bandares peeked inside.

"She's the most beautiful woman I've ever seen my entire life!" He thought, staring in awe at the slightly heavy set, almond brown-skinned woman whose luscious lips were coated in a glossy, yet hypnotizing blue lipstick - the same color as her hair and makeup.

Moving closer to take in her details, he could see her thick curvy body gracefully moving about in her Imperial armour as she lovingly and meticulously wiped down Nepson's nude body.

"Nepson's body is with her and not with the unit commanders?" He thought, stealing glances at her crystal clear blue eyes whenever her long curly blue hair afforded him the chance.

"With whom? Please don't say you want me to bear children with these men; from what I've seen of this group, all but ten are completely useless. Correction, they're useful for fodder when real warriors like myself need diversions and bodies to throw at the enemy to wear down numbers and resources."

The woman's words stung him to the core, and he immediately jumped to the conclusion that he wasn't one of the men she'd described, especially since he knew at some point she'd come to his chamber's and collected Nepson's body.

"She could've easily left Nepson for our unit commanders, but she must've thought I was so pathetic she'd rather take on soul sending duties than lay with me," he thought, feeling a lump of sorrow rise in his throat.

"I smell pre-come and nervous sweat. Whoever's hiding behind that pillar over there, better get their ass in here now!" The woman commanded, causing him to jump out of his skin in surprise.

For the first time in his life he found himself wanting to defy a woman, but it didn't matter because his feet had already betrayed him.

Chapter II

Under Imminent threat

Imperial Date: 1676 ABCAE
Ah Tabai Date: 384 cycles after ceding from Adrasteia

Location: Adrasteia binary solar system.
Moon-world of Ah Tabai, which is seventh of fourteen habitable moon-worlds
orbiting the Gas giant Tepeu

Ah Tabai leadership: World government of the Matriarchy
Population: Forty-four billion

WA'RAYDON'S HEART WAS BEATING OUT of his chest watching his home planet of Ah Tabai appear through the viewport of Tier ten, Void Assault Admiral Botatu's voidship as it settled into orbit.

"I had to watch my children born on holo-imager and I haven't seen my family for a full cycle! I wish this debrief would end already!"

"And that's why we need Tier four, Void Assault Admiral Wa'raydon to walk to the nearest airlock and space himself," Wa'raydon heard suddenly.

"Huh?" Wa'raydon muttered, jumping in his seat in surprise just as everyone in the briefing chamber burst into laughter.

"Care to pay attention Wa'raydon?" Admiral Botatu said, giving him a playful mocking look of annoyance.

"I'm all ears," Wa'raydon replied, placing his hands behind his ears as he extended portions of his helmet armor implants around his ears.

"He's so pale, short and scrawny, maybe he's already freeze dried void meat," he heard a woman slip in through the laughter.

"Hey I'm not short! Seven foot three is the lower limit for an average height man of Ah Tabai! And I'm not scrawny, today I weighed in at three hundred twenty pounds, thank you very much."

"Maybe we'd notice but we can't see you half the time. As a matter of fact, I've had breast milk darker than you," another woman chimed in.

"Ah, it's genetic, it's genetic, and besides my mom is one of those blue star haters. She's always like, let's get in, let's get in, blue light is coming out, so give me a break. If I start catching rays now, I'll be just as dark as Admiral Botatu," Wa'raydon said, bobbing his head at Botatu as he shifted in his seat so he could have a better angle to see out the viewport closest to him.

"Oh, we can't see him either, he's the same color as the void itself," a man piped out.

"And just as scrawny as Wa'raydon," a woman said right after.

"Hey, hey, I thought we were all making fun of Wa'raydon, not me. But I see some of you want extra duty," Botatu said, chuckling darkly.

"Wa'raydon, aren't your mates just as tall as you?" A woman asked, sounding as if she were about to lose her composure at the mere thought of it.

"Can't I just look at the planet in peace? Leave my mates out of this," he said, already knowing more than half the Admirals in the chamber were going to call up images of himself and his two mates to do a size comparison now that someone had brought it up.

"Yhea, his Re'meka is one inch shorter, and his Adenetta is two inches shorter. Aww and look, he found two women like his parents. Re'meka is honey-brown like his mother, and Adenetta is light-cream color like his father," he heard the woman sitting directly behind him say.

"Isn't there a name for people who pick mates that resemble their parents? I think it's some kind of complex. What's the name of it again? Oh seven lives, it's at the tip of my tongue. Oh! I think its Oedipus complex or something like that. Yhea his mates are short like his parents. See, his mom is only six foot nine and his dad is the same height as him."

"Okay, okay, I'll pay attention! Seven lives, the lot of you can turn a surreal home coming into a nightmare!" Wa'raydon proclaimed, unable to stop himself from laughing as he shifted his body that much more towards the nearest viewport.

"Wa'raydon I'm over here," he heard Botatu say.

"I said I'd pay attention, I never said I wouldn't look out the view port," Wa'raydon said, turning only his head towards Botatu.

Admiral Botatu smiled and shook his head, then all the view ports in the chamber closed.

"Aww," Wa'raydon proclaimed sarcastically, causing everyone to crack up laughing again.

"All right, pay attention, I know that was a long deployment and everyone wants to go home. But just a little while ago, some disturbing Intel came in that our good old friends, the Adrasteia Empire, have been increasing their hostile posture towards the forty-eight independent moon-worlds.

"Oh come on, not this crap again. Adrasteia has neither the people nor the resources to take back this system. And the Adrasteia binary moon-worlds have been independent for well over three hundred cycles. As a matter of fact, who's even truly loyal to Adrasteia anymore?

Heka system shouldn't count - they're a total joke, even with all those people living on their forty-six moon-worlds. Most of them would rather pray and chant to those disgusting, vulgar Goddesses all day rather than fight anyone. And the Kampana system...please, they're no threat. If anything, they're worse than the Heka system people with all that praying and chanting. And..."

"And what do you have to say about Adrasteia's still loyal and willing R'yu system? Or what about the people from the Yin't and Yin'n system? Just because you haven't heard much about them, doesn't mean they're inactive. As a matter of fact, it's quite the contrary. Since both systems annex five hundred cycles ago, they're the ones who've been truly serving as Adrasteia's second and third point of the trident," Admiral Botatu said calmly cutting him off, during which time Wa'raydon could see multiple holo-imagers springing to life, displaying Adrasteia's controlled solar systems.

Wa'raydon grit his teeth as he took in the details of Adrasteia binary solar system, wishing the independent people of the forty-eight moon-worlds would finally come up with a better name than the 'Adrasteia binary system.'

"Right now, the nature of our binary solar system has put the forty eight moon-worlds at a disadvantage. As all of you can see, all three Gas giants belonging to our binary system, along with the forty-eight moon-worlds that orbit them, are beginning the solar system swap between our Red giant and Blue giant star. And as you can see, our Gas giant Tepeu is going to be first to cross close orbits with Adrasteia during this swap. There's also another situation tied into this swap scenario that's more concerning, but I'll wait for one of you to figure it out and tell me," Botatu said, folding his hands behind his back.

Wa'raydon stared fixedly at the holographic display, first looking at Tepeu with its fourteen moon-worlds, including his home moon-world of Ah Tabai. Then at Gas giant Thoth with its twenty-five moon-worlds. And finally at Tezcatlipoca with its nine moon-worlds. Biting the inside of his lip, he couldn't help himself but smile.

"Something you want to get off your chest Wa'raydon?" Botatu asked, and to Wa'raydon it seemed like Botatu already knew what he was thinking.

"We should unify and squash Adrasteia as we pass. What do they have? A population of seventy billon max? Two trillion against seventy billion seems like excellent odds to me."

"Really? Are you adding yourself, your family and almost everyone you know and care about into your equation? Sixty billion of Adrasteia's population are citizens whom are battle-tested and war-ready. Roughly five billion are slaves, itching for a chance to prove their worth in order to become citizens.

The rest are literally infants and young children below the age of twelve, of both slave and citizen alike, who are equally ready to fight and die just to prove themselves worthy to the Empire and their family. Can you imagine being blown to bits in the void by a ten cycle-old? How could you face any of us in your next life?" Botatu asked, with a sinister grin.

Shaking his head at Botatu, Wa'raydon said, "Still seems like good odds to me," not liking the idea of Botatu coaxing him into being afraid of people coming from what he considered to be an old washed-up Empire.

"Really? Still think so huh? How about this. It's estimated if just the military force from the planet Adrasteia itself attacked all the moon-worlds orbiting our Gas giant simultaneously, of the fourteen moon-worlds, only two would retain a population worth Adrasteia enslaving. This estimation is based on Adrasteia's standard Tier one, no-mercy-for-all attack, which usually last one hundred days. Can you imagine if they decided to extend that to one hundred fifty days or even two hundred? If that happened, all fourteen moon-worlds orbiting this Gas giant would literally become sterile."

"Yes but the Adrasteian's losses…"

"Let me finish Wa'raydon. But yes, many wanted to revel in the idea of the Adrasteian's taking high casualties as well. So the powers that be did some scenario number crunching to estimate what the Adrasteian's casualty rate would look like within those same one hundred days. The scenarios involved were always based on if all fourteen moon-worlds fought their hardest, using every single resource at their disposal. Unfortunately, the end calculation was the planetary force of Adrasteia losing maybe a quarter of their people. Though, I personally think that's a gross overestimation."

"Yes, but if the moon-worlds unify for this effort!" Wa'raydon began.

"The moon-worlds unify!? It's been three hundred and eight-four cycles since we ceded from Adrasteia and in that time we haven't even come up with a name for this binary solar system. We don't even have proper trade agreements with the two moon-worlds on either side of our orbit yet! How do you think we'll fare when it comes to uniting a proper military force?"

"With all due respect Admiral Botatu, isn't that what we already have at the blockade of the two thousand entanglement points? All the moon-worlds send ships and supplies as well as coordinate with each other," Wa'raydon said, envisioning what life must be like for the billions of people manning voidbases and voidships at the entanglement points.

"You're too young and have never been to the blockades, so you can't fathom the truth Wa'raydon. What you're thinking is not there."

"Please tell me then, what is there?" He asked, genuinely wanting to know.

"Organised chaos, a pissing contest with billions of kunusses and kudocks firing every which way, not even able to agree on which way the piss should go in order to choose a winner. A logistical nightmare, where for cycles on end, supplies and ammunition rarely ever arrive. When something finally does arrive, it usually comes in overabundance and is usually utterly useless.

Such as when my voidbase received a shipment of fifty trillion metric tons of tasteless and non-nutritional gwapla fruit! In the seven lives! They can't even agree on a Fleet Admiral to lead the blockade if the Adrasteian's were ever smart enough to try and reuse these points. Smart, because Adrasteia could float a ten billion person strong armada by and everyone would be too damn busy arguing to even notice them! In short, all the moon-worlds would end up fighting this war alone. Sorry to end your fantasy Wa'raydon, but life would be better if…Ah! Never mind!"

Wa'raydon's feelings of superiority over Adrasteia sank every second he listened to Botatu. Not wanting to make eye contact with him after he'd finished speaking, he stared at the holo-imager.

That's odd, he thought as his mind did calculations of the stars and planets future trajectories.

From his calculations, he could see that a strange gravitational event was beginning to take place. The two stars that normally orbited approximately four light days apart would come as close as one and a half light days apart. During that time, he noticed they'd lose their steady orbit about each other and begin a wild end over end tumble, disrupting the orbits of the planetary bodies belonging to the binary system.

Unnerving as this situation was, he could see that the planets weren't in any immediate danger and that they were still going to complete the swap between the two stars. However, this is where he realised the magnetic fields in the system would be interacting on a whole new level of intensity as the stars aligned themselves one on top of the other.

'Oh crap!' Wa'raydon whispered, realising that every single planet in the binary system would be positioned over or between the magnetic poles of the stars during the exact moment of their alinement.

"All two thousand entanglement blockade points will mean nothing in a half cycle's time. The planet swap is causing a gravity imbalance and the two solar systems are beginning to tumble about each other. Naturally forming entanglement points of enormous strength will be at Adrasteia's fingertips as it crosses directly in-between both solar systems' connected magnetic fields.

Even if we can use the naturally forming entanglement points, they'll have the advantage because they'll be using Kampana crystals and Heka metals to keep the entanglement points stabilized to a greater degree than we can achieve. Without knowing where the points will open in relation to us, there's no way we could set up a feasible defense too far away from Ah Tabai. We'd have to hunker down around the planet and wait for them to come. Damn it! This is a pre-war briefing isn't it?" He blurted out, feeling butterflies in his stomach.

"Wa'raydon, always the sharp one. How many of you had already figured this out, without having to do the equations in their head?" Botatu asked sarcastically, causing everyone in the chamber to raise their hand and send him playful looks.

"Now that I've eased our slowest Admiral into the bad news, let's talk about what we need to do to prepare for their arrival. As all of you have seen, the tumble of the stars has already begun. The process will go fast and slow. Fast because the more they slip into the tumble, the faster they'll go. Slow because this tumble is calculated to last between two hundred and four hundred cycles. I am afraid that when the Adrasteians come, none of us will live long enough to see the completion of our two suns' awkward dance."

For the rest of the three hour briefing, Wa'raydon barely listened unless it had something to do with evacuating families or what part his unit would play in the orbit-guard of his planet. When he felt he could sit no longer, Wa'raydon asked the question he'd been holding onto since he realised he was attending a war briefing.

"Admiral, can we see our families or are we stuck up here, never to see them again as we wait for Adrasteia to attack? I mean, can we at least go down there to help our loved ones get settled in the shelters ships?"

"If I say no, all of you are going to ignore me and go down there anyway. In the seven lives, if the top said no to me, I'd still go down there anyway. With that being said, manning orders are being uploaded to your implants as I speak. We trust you young Admirals to delineate these orders to your lessers properly. Please take a few minutes to do so now."

After two minutes, Wa'raydon had finished organising time slots for the five hundred thousand Void Assault personnel under his command. After reading the roster, he was annoyed that he along with the other Admirals in the briefing chamber were prescheduled to return to the ship.

"Admiral, why do we have to come back here tomorrow? So we can plan to plan, then plan some more? Everyone here knows these pre-war plans are hypothetical. In the three hours we've been here, we've already covered all the various ways to defend our world.

I'd understand if we're coming here tomorrow to discuss the other moon-worlds, but if we're not adding them to our plans, then I really don't get it. Especially since you've already made it clear that none of the other moon-worlds are truly going to work together. And not to sound like I have little faith in our planets combat pros, but wouldn't our government just simply surrender to keep us from being sacked? We'll all be slaves for a few cycles, then we'd start at Tier one all over again. Right?"

Wa'raydon felt anxious after asking the question mostly because he was serious. After hours of hearing all the different ways everyone in the forty eight moon-worlds should expect doom, gloom and death, he figured giving up could possibly be in everyone's best interest.

"Unfortunately, your innocent mind hasn't figured it out yet. Adrasteia doesn't like to take on adults as slaves, it takes too much time and energy to brainwash an adult. And even then, there's a big risk that said adult could have a sudden lapse in loyalty. Hence their notorious use of Tier one siege attacks.

On your way to the surface, I implore all of you to upload historic documentaries of our former rulers' tactics, strategies and belief systems. I have a feeling many of you will be returning to the ship much sooner than tomorrow once you see how awful these people are. Okay kids, that's all I have for you till tomorrow. Wa'raydon, stay for a moment. I'd like to have a word with you," Botatu said wearily, giving Wa'raydon the feeling he'd finally rubbed him the wrong way with his outburst.

As the chamber cleared, Wa'raydon made his way down the small stairway that lead to the center of the chamber where Botatu stood.

"Hey, I'm sorry, I didn't mean…," Wa'raydon started to say.

"Do you think I care about your immature outburst at this point?" Botatu said so flatly Wa'raydon found himself questioning whether he'd just received an attack or a compliment.

"You called me here…"

"I called you here because I want to ask you for a personal favor, which is to put that brain of yours to work on a few math equations derived by some of Ah Tabai's, umm- greatest alchemic scientist."

Wa'raydon was confused at the question for more than a few reasons, but decided not to ask anything when he saw the weary look on Botatu's face turn to one of hopelessness.

"Sure thing," he responded, bobbing his head, hoping he looked reassuring.

"Thank you. It'll only hurt a bit okay, I'd say maybe a similar pain as your body armor implants."

"Hey that's not a little. Ahh, seven lives this hurts! And this is not a few!" He proclaimed through gritted teeth as Botatu uploaded the data.

In less than a second, hundreds of thousands of mathematical equations mixed with sacred geometric patterns had already floated before his eyes, making him giddy with anticipation to solve them.

"It's a little bit of a secret that I have these calculations, understand? I trust your blabber mouth is strictly for nonsense so I'm personally trusting you with this. If anyone catches brain waves from you or sees this from a slip in your implant filtering, just say it's some research you're working on when you noticed the solar system tumble.

Everyone expects a jumble of math in your head anyway. If they poke around in the first thousand or so equations, that's all they're going to see anyway. But just to be certain everything stays unreadable to others, you're going to have to de-organize each equation after you've solved it, which is the main reason I'm giving them to you. I'm very confident in your ability to deduce the big picture from a vast number of smaller ones."

"If something slips through my implant settings or if someone, umm sees some of my brain waves. Won't they still be able to see the smaller images?" Wa'raydon asked apprehensively.

"Read the message, crumble it up, and repeat. The interpreted message goes to a different, less accessible part of your brain. And don't forget to watch the uncensored documentaries of how Adrasteia gained control of both the R'yu and the Yin't and Yin'n systems."

"I will, I mean, I won't. I mean, I will do my best to do as you say Admiral," Wa'raydon stammered, feeling overwhelmed.

When he could finally see straight, Botatu was already walking up one of the slender staircases that ran throughout the circular chamber.

"If all goes well, I'll see you soon Wa'raydon. Be sure to make love to your two mates like it'll be your last... it very well could be," Botatu said softly just before walking through a round blast door at the top of the stairs.

"No one needs to tell me that. I for certain will," he thought, bounding up a set of stairs in the opposite direction.

Once he was out of the meeting chamber, it only took him thirty seconds to reach a single-person pod launch location. Wasting no time, he hopped into the opening of the spherical voidship, then extended his consciousness outward.

"Electro symbioses ten percent, merge initiate," Wa'raydon mentally commanded almost unconsciously.

Within a tenth of a second, millions of alchemically created nano-filaments resembling fiber optics fired out of his spine, connecting him to the ship.

"Launch," he commanded with his mind.

Less than a second later, he felt the slightest touch of G pressure before his ship's anti G technology kicked in, leaving only fluttering sensations in his stomach as his voidship smoothly accelerated through the half mile long tube. Entering into the void after the third second, Wa'raydon instantly felt his mind at ease. To him, being alone in the void was like a home away from home.

"Three hundred and sixty full view," Wa'raydon mentally commanded, enabling him to see everything in every direction simultaneously.

"Almost nothing is this beautiful and almost nothing is this exhilarating," he mumbled as his tiny one-man orb began to enter the atmosphere of his planet.

With ease and finesse, he adjusted his trajectory, lining himself up with his home city. Once that was done, he logged himself in with the mega building his family lived within. Then for most of the remaining ten minute flight, he worked on the calculations Botatu had uploaded while staring at the nearly perfect merge of nature and technology covering his entire home planet.

"Hey son! We were wondering when you were going to get down here." Wa'raydon heard his father say over his ship's coms as he approached his family unit on the four hundredth level of the Mega building.

"Ah! You always keep half your consciousness in the landing logs! You ruin surprises!" Wa'raydon said aloud as the tree that grew symbiotically with the building opened a budding leaf for his voidship to land on.

"Looks like even the tree missed me," Wa'raydon said, chuckling as he aimed his orb in the middle of the leaf aglow with a warm array of soft welcoming colors.

Landing gently, he disconnected from the ship and rushed out onto the thick leaf to find his family rushing out to greet him. His father was the first to hug him. Behind his father, he could see his mother cradling two newborn babies.

"Are you two trying to populate the moon-world all on your own?" He asked playfully while moving past his father to kiss his mother on the cheek and forehead.

A short distance behind his mother, he saw his two mates standing inside the unit just shy of the leaf balcony holding two infants each.

"Ha! Who am I to talk," he chuckled, giving his mother another kiss on the forehead before approaching the two women he spent most of his waking moments thinking about.

Seeing their warm genuine smiles, he desperately wanted to embrace them, but he could instantly see it wasn't going to be possible.

"They're already just like daddy, wanting all the attention," he whispered, watching his son and three daughters as they nursed.

"Hey you…we missed you," Adenetta said, readying her lips for a kiss.

Kissing her, he smoothly moved his kiss to Re'meka, then stood back and looked at them, then at his children again.

"It's been far too long. I wish I'd never signed up for this rotation," he whispered, feeling tears well up in his eyes as he thought about all the big and small moments he'd missed out on, feeling guilty that he had to watch all four of his children born via holo-imager.

"Come all the way in children, blue light will touch soon and I don't want the babies out in it," his mother said in a sweet voice, pressing the back of his torso-armor.

"And un-form your armor sweetie. You're home now, so get naked," Adenetta said, playfully shaking her head.

"Oh! Right!" He said, withdrawing his armor into his body, leaving him nude.

The look on Adenetta and Re'meka's face said it all. Not needing to say even a word after entering the apartment, his parents calmly took the children, and the women not so calmly took him to the pleasure chamber. After hours of love-making, he lay between them and softly began to sob as powerful waves of emotion coursed through him.

"Hey sweetie? What's wrong? Re'meka asked, kissing him softly on the cheek, making him want to cry even harder.

"How do explain the mix of emotion I feel? I don't even know why I'm crying," Wa'raydon thought as he forced his mind to put labels on each emotion.

"I'm happy," he mumbled.

Adenetta inched her body over his even more so and began kissing his other cheek.

"I'm the happiest I ever remember being. Seeing the two of you, the children, my parents and my brother and sister," Wa'raydon said, feeling more tears running down his cheeks while catching the subtle scents of his favorite dish being prepared by his parents.

Trying to swallow the lump in his throat, he opened his mouth, but didn't want to say his next words.

"And I'm also sad, the saddest I've ever been in my entire life. I think... I think all of us are going to die, very, very soon."

Saying it aloud, Wa'raydon felt the mental dam keeping him from all out sobbing disintegrate, allowing him to cry unhindered until he felt utterly exhausted.

"Okay, that's enough of that," he muttered, sitting up in the bed made of soft-leaf lined with La'rick worm silk.

Wondering why the women had yet to say one playful thing about his sudden outburst, he turned around anticipating to see sarcastic pouty faces, only to find their faces wrought with sorrow and eyes glossed over with unshed tears.

"I take it while I was receiving the briefing in the void, the government was briefing everyone down here?"

Wrapping her arms around him, Adenetta whispered, "Well, not in so many words. In the last few months, the world government has been hinting there's imminent danger, but not from who or what. Upping the propaganda for procreation, then upping the commercials about evacuation safety. And for the last ten days, every single commercial is: Do you know your evacuation route? Is your family prepared for natural disasters? And just before you arrived, there was a commercial asking 'when was the last time you checked your shelter ship's system and supplies',"

"I'm sorry ladies, I shouldn't have brought this up. I'm ruining our relax time," he replied softly, running his hand down Adenetta's back while rubbing Re'meka's leg.

"Eww, your cum is cold, don't rub it on my leg." Re'meka said chuckling, which to Wa'raydon sounded somewhat forced.

"That's definitely not my cum, we all know for certain where most of that is," he said mockingly, feeling the strange, cold, thick and sticky texture on her leg, wondering what could feel like that if it weren't his cum or theirs.

"It leaks out of us smart one," Adenetta said, resting her head on his shoulder as she hugged him tighter.

"Yea, but this isn't mine," Wa'raydon whispered, feeling the same texture drip onto his back.

"Hey? That feels gross. What is that? Oh no!" Adenetta said in a hushed voice, lifting her head off his shoulder, staring at the tree branches and vines running over their heads.

"What is it?" He asked, looking up to see branches and vines oozing viscous pink sap.

"OH! Seven Lives! Mom! Dad!" He screamed, jumping up and running towards his parents and children in the kitchen next to the open balcony.

"Get aw-" The infinitesimal vibration through his feet, the sick feeling in his stomach, and the stillness in the air, all combined to make the seconds it took him to make it to the threshold of the pleasure chamber feel like an eternity.

It was in this eternity he somehow managed to turn his head to the left as he came out, just in time to see a kinetic warhead go off in the heart of his city, twenty-five miles away. Even from that distance, he was able to feel the first searing hot shock wave run across his body...

Chapter III

Worthless

ROUNDING THE PILLAR, BANDARES forced his fear down so that as he walked into the Temple, it felt the same as when he entered the Ba Gua Zhang circle during combat training.

"I knew I recognised your scent Tier one Bandares. Are you here to see me? Or to pray before we set off. If you're here to see me, there's no need. I'll be addressing all of you shortly," the blue-haired woman said casually, not even looking up from Nepson's body as she cleaned it.

Bandares mind raced trying to understand what she was talking about.

"I came to pray for guidance. I feel lost and confused about my life. However, I'll gladly serve you if you so wish," Bandares said, feeling a smoldering anger starting to grow from the bottom of his diaphragm.

"You don't care about me at all? You left me alone. Alienating me. Giving more reason for everyone to treat me like crap," he thought.

"If you're here for clarity, don't let me stop you from praying. Just make sure you're in the briefing chamber at the allotted time. By the way, you're still wearing your slave clothing, take those raged pants off and leave them here," the woman said looking up, giving Bandares the first full view of her beautiful almond-brown face, spotted with slight darker freckles.

Looking deep into her clear blue eyes as she looked up at him, he felt the small erection that'd been growing since he'd caught wind of the sixty-four Yogini priestesses' kunusses grow even stronger.

"Is there anything you'd like to say to me that you think I might not address during the briefing?" The woman asked, keeping her eyes locked on him as she pressed the temple floor.

Below her fingers, sacred geometric patterns began to form under

Nepson's body. Seconds later, Nepson's muscular body was floating up right. Seeing the ridged body, Bandares shook his head in disbelief at the cruelty he'd been shown, and felt annoyed at himself for not being able to save his life.

"If I may speak freely?" He asked, slightly averting his gaze from the woman.

"Sure," The woman said standing up as she cast the final petrification spell on Nepson's body.

Watching the body turn to stone and return to the ground, he believed for a moment he'd actually witnessed Nepson's soul leaving the body. This sent him into a daydream of what he thought his next life might be like.

"Hey short one! What'd you want to say?" The woman asked impatiently, shattering his thoughts.

"Oh, um. I just feel like he deserved more respect. He was always nice and always kept to himself, and in the end, not even the unit commanders came to retrieve his body. I feel like they left him there like trash."

"Humm. You think your unit commanders left him there? Bandares, do you know the nature of the brain worm? And on another note, now that I'm truly paying attention to you, I realise the preliminary citizen implants you received the day before aren't working."

Bandares asked his implants for time and location and both appeared in his mind's eye.

"Oh…umm, is there a way to-"

"What's my name?"

"I don't…I don't know…I don't see anything when I look at you, but I thought it's because-"

"My name is Tier four, Ground Assault Elite General Tara. I'm your new unit commander. Your new implants should've told you this as well as given you a short debrief on your status change from slave to citizen.

The debrief would've also broken down how Tier levels work in the Empire, but I think I know why your implants aren't working. You were born on R'yu as a slave, living in the slums next to the sewers that run into the Kawaya no kami sludge river, correct?"

"Yes, yes I was," Bandares said, trying to anticipate her point, as well as figure out what she meant by asking him if he knew the true nature of the brain worm.

"You played in the sludge, ate in the sludge, did everything in the sludge, so you must remember the times when you saw the silver and black stuff moving in the water. It looked like mercury or dark oily metal. And just as you started to stare at it, it'd disappear right?"

"Yhea," Bandares whispered, recalling exactly what she was describing.

"I see. I'll have to take care of your implants personally. I had a similar problem growing up in a slave village, next to a polluted ocean on my home planet of Yin'n. I'm afraid praying here will do you no good as it won't clear up the problem with your implants. On another note, when it comes to prayer in general, you shouldn't pray here anyway. I just didn't feel like being bothered mentioning this to you earlier.

You're no longer a slave who serves the Empire and its ways, but a citizen who follows the Empire's guidance. I know it sounds the same, but there's a big difference. For one thing, you'll start to see the social dynamics between men and women change drastically. Where you once had to grovel before every woman, you need now only show endearing respect."

"Endearing respect, yes unit commander. Your will be done, my life is to be of your service."

"Ah, calm down - showing endearing respect is not exactly mandatory, only do this on case by case basis, as you'll soon find many women aren't... never mind you'll see for yourself in the next few hours. Anyway, if you need clarity, it should come from your female peers first. If your situation hasn't been alleviated by them, only then should you seek guidance from a Temple."

"Two women I ran into a few minutes ago told me they would've aided me in prayer if they'd had their cycles. At the time, I didn't understand. I'd never heard of it. I just didn't want to ask because I was sca-, because I saw they were really busy."

"Sure Bandares," Tara replied sarcastically, raising her eyebrows in doubt.

"Yhea because I," he wanted to tell another small lie, but the 'whatever you say' face she made as he tried to think of something, changed his mind and made him decide to stay on topic.

"So, are you saying that all women on their cycles can serve as priestesses?" He asked, thinking, *"that's why they behaved so oddly when I groveled before them. They must've thought I ignored my implants debriefing and had chosen to grovel anyway."*

"Yes," Tara said flatly, squatting and pulling down his ragged pants, exposing his erect kudock.

"Your pre-cum smells stale," she said, taking his kudock into her mouth sending shivers up his spine.

As his kudock slid deeper into her mouth, she began to massage his testis while working her head back and forth in long slow motions that quickly made him feel like he was about to cum. Gasping for breath, he moved himself back, embarrassed and slightly fearful he was about to release in her mouth so quickly.

Making a sound of disappointment as his kudock slipped out of her mouth, she looked up with an evil glare that made his heart skip a few beats.

"And it taste disgusting. Aboard the transport voidship your diet will be regulated," she said in a neutral tone that didn't match the emotions he saw playing across her face.

Bandares couldn't think straight and he couldn't help but question why she'd done what she had. In the few seconds that'd passed, her face had changed from anger to mischievous intent, in which she was now smirking at the long thick stream of pre-cum trailing from the tip of his kudock.

"You don't think I'm worthless? You left me alone in the chamber while all the other…"

"I think many men are worthless. Are you worthless Bandares?" Tara said, standing up quickly.

As she stood, he watched her face go from mischievous to emotionless all within the blink of an eye. Staring at her, he groped for the right words to explain how he felt about himself. Desperate to say anything, seeing that she'd begun to clinch her jaw over and over, he decided to say exactly how he felt without bending the truth.

"I heard what you said to the priestesses…"

"Well, maybe you shouldn't listen to other's conversations. Yes Bandares, I left you because I thought you're worthless. Are you happy with my answer?"

Bandares hadn't felt the eyes of the priestesses till she'd said those words. Now, he felt as if all sixty-four of them were watching him, laughing at him and mocking him. Looking at the nude women sitting around the temple in crystalline chairs with their legs spread open so that their cycles could drip freely from their kunusses, he felt like he could commit suicide right then and there.

"If I can, can I do anything to be of worth?" Bandares stammered.

"Shut up. No, don't shut up. Tell me, what's the nature of the brain worm, Bandares? I want to hear your worthless mind working."

"The… the brain worms first enter your body through mucous membranes."

"Okay…and they come from where?"

"From the shattered worlds' debris. The unit leaders. Um, my old unit leaders said they were ancient worms that could live in stasis inside the rocks, awaking if they made contact with a living world or being. And that sometimes they were…"

"Long story short Banderas, the worms live in debris. Mainly in the debris cluster where your friend who beat you half to death originates from. And it just so happens, his clan is locked in war with Nepson and U'te'el's debris clan. You ever heard of parasite hosting during war? Or maybe vector warfare. Using viruses' bacteria and or parasites to infect the enemy?"

Bandares shivered even at the mere thought of it before saying, "No."

"Nepson was nice and quiet because Nepson was nicely and quietly having his way with his enemies at night, including your friend 'lord ass kick.' Their two clans have been fighting, degrading, and killing each other for thousands of cycles and no subjugation under the same Imperial rule will ever stop them.

Hosting brain worms and other vectors in the body is just one of the many tricks the debris' clans use to kill people. So after countless times being infected by all the people he was having his way with, Nepson's immune system finally failed.

And look at the ridges on Nepson's kudock, he was using a different type of parasite to infect his enemies. So what do you think of the man you were speaking so highly of now, now that you know he was willing to risk his life, all just to harm another person?"

Bandares looked over at Nepson statued body, taking in the small pock marks around the width of his kudock and found himself shuttering again.

"You're naive and worthless Bandares, and I really don't think you're going to make it in my brigade. Whenever I look at you, the first thing I think is that you're as soft as the inside of a whore's kunuss. I can't believe you'd think I'd want to lay under someone like you. I'd never take a weakling like you inside of me Bandares.

"I…I,"

"I, I what? And don't look at me like that. What, you think you're a man because you have man parts? As a matter of fact, I changed my mind, you shouldn't seek your female peers for clarity. Based on the context of your slave mindset, the temples are the only place you belong."

With each sentence, Bandares watched her anger grow until she was breathing so heavily it appeared as if her skin-tight, bio-mechanical body armor were going to rip off of her torso. Seeing her in that state made him want to yell at her, to tell her that he wasn't worthless, to explain his perspective. But every time he opened his mouth to speak, she'd glare at him with a look he interpreted as intent to kill.

"I'll do as you bid unit leader," Bandares finally managed to choke out.

Looking downward, he began to waddle over to some of the nearest Yogini priestesses with his ragged pants still wrapped around his ankles. Looking up at them for reassurance, he could see they weren't even looking at him, but at Tara behind him, which somehow furthered his belief that he was worthless. When some of their eyes finally did fall upon him, all he could see was pity. But before he could even break eye contact, he felt something rock hard slam against the back of his head.

In that moment he felt his entire body shut down, giving him the sensation of weightlessness. While his vision went dark around the edges, he was able to make out Tara's body armor as she moved in front of him. That's when he knew without truly feeling her touch, that she'd caught him before he'd hit the ground.

"I have to stop letting my guard down," he thought fuzzily as his blurry vision returned to normal, where he could see he was now laying in-between Tara's legs.

He could hear her mumbling something incoherent over and over. Straining his ears, he finally heard her say, "When a woman goes down and sucks your disgusting tasting......she obviously likes...stupid......understands nothing...women."

"What am I supposed to understand? A woman's word is absolute. I'm really confused," he thought, feeling his motor functions returning.

"This is going to hurt, but it must be done. Keep still until I tell you to drink my cycle. Am I clear?" He heard her say as he felt something searing hot dig into the back of his neck.

"Ahhh!" He screamed as the pain traveled through his neck into his head and down his spine.

"O shut up," he heard her mumbled through his screams.

As the pain began to subside, jumbled glyphs started forming in his mind. Soon after, Banderas could see his name, title and Tier rank in the upper right hand corner of his mind's eye.

"You should be able to see something now. Is it coherent?"

"I see Tier one Bandares. And I see a sacred geometric pattern that looks like a torus and a nautilus shell all in one,"

"Oh, good then. You don't need any cycle blood yet. Okay get up, on your feet, let's go," Tara said hurriedly as she hopped up, leaving the back of his neck feeling raw and exposed.

"I don't think I can stan-," he started to say as an image of a chamber filling with men from his unit and many others appeared in his mind's eye.

"Tier one Bandares, you are required to attend citizenships inauguration ceremony in meeting chamber of Yogini's love in ten minutes. The Adrasteia Empire welcomes you to her arms. Unit commander is Tier four, Ground Assault Elite General Tara," scrolled across his mind's eye with an image of Tara appearing on top of the live stream feed from the inauguration chamber.

"Your current Tier status can be elevated upon completion of specific duties as well as common duties. Please refer to promotional duties section for further details," appeared after the image of Tara, with a flashing icon annotating the section he should read.

"Oh really? You're just going to lay there and read?" Tara growled and before he could move, he felt himself snatched up and flung over her shoulder.

"Do you get what you're reading or are you too dumb? Just in case you're dumb, when we're on the voidship, task indicators will tell you things you can do to improve your Tier. As a matter of fact, when you look at me, an indication will show you that combat practice with me is something you can do as well. Please come fight me before you get your worthless ass killed," she said flinging him to the ground while simultaneously snatching off his ragged pants.

"Why should I wait!?" Bandares thought, standing up and balling his fist.

"Oh? You want to go now?" She asked chucking his pants into his chest.

Seeing the look of malice on her face, he quickly changed his mind.

"Even if I wanted to, I will not," he said, un-balling his fist trying to discreetly steal a glance behind him, wondering if he could make a run for it if she'd decided to initiate the fight.

"Why? You're allowed to fight a woman since you're no longer slave. As a citizen, if you injure or attack another and they're capable of regaining justice for themselves, then it matters not if it's man or woman. There's no outside punishment for the person who has claimed retribution against the initiator, and no outside punishment for the initiator once the retribution is claimed. So, strike me as you please. Or should I say try to."

As she spoke, Bandares watched her open a blast door he'd never been authorised to pass through as a slave. Smiling, she began to walk through and just before she fully crossed the threshold, she indicated with her index finger for him to follow.

"I don't think I want to follow her, I feel like she is going to swing the moment I step through the door."

"I'm not going to hit you. If I was going to, you wouldn't be standing right now. I just wanted to see your reaction to my challenge. Come, I don't want to be late."

"Fair enough," he thought, walking through the door.

As they walked down the passageway, his implants were firing off all sorts of arbitrary information ranging from Tara's age, the new diet he was to follow, as well as the first documented encounters the Adrasteia Empire had with the brain worms.

"My implants are driving me crazy. What did you do to me? And why am I, along with the rest of the men nude?" He asked annoyed, feeling dizzy as his implants streamed more and more information across his field of vision, almost to the point where he couldn't see the ground in front of him.

"You go from crawling to running. One minute you're scared to speak to women, now you're riddling me with questions like I'm your equal. Hummm."

Bandares felt a small pang of fear rise in his chest, realising his tone toward her was disrespectful. But his fear was quickly quashed when she ever so slightly turned and touched his head. The moment she did, all the images disappeared.

"Tha-Thank you," he mumbled, feeling relieved.

"I didn't do enough if you're having a hard time filtering, but I'll deal with it when we're in the void. You're already becoming a pain in my ass…going to be late to my own meeting because of you."

"How's that an answer for what you actually did? Don't you think I deserve to know what's wrong with my implants? You're just as selfish as they are," Banderas muttered, thinking of the slave unit he'd spent the last ten cycles of his life with.

"I'm selfish? Really? I'm the one who saved your life, not the regrowth gel you put in your lungs. When I arrived, you were almost the same color as my hair. And your implants wouldn't have ever worked if you'd been assigned to another brigade other than mine.

And it's not because people in the other brigades couldn't help you, it's because they'd make wagers on the way you'd become a corpse due to your implants failing to tell you there's danger. Seven Lives! To call me selfish! You know, I was even going to trigger my painful ass cycle for you to drink if it came down to it. Be careful who you call selfish."

"Then why!? Why are you calling me worthless, then helping me!? And if we're being honest, what power do women's cycles have? I never felt clarity taking in cycle blood. It just smells fishy and somehow still makes me hard! That's about it! No magic, no nothing! Unless the power is to cause me to have wet dreams, I don't get it!"

Bandares hadn't known where the last part had come from. He'd only meant to talk about her, but when she'd brought up triggering her cycle, he didn't want her to be able to hold something over him he thought was worthless. Seeing her turn around fully with a maniacal look on her face, Bandares was sure if he still had even an ounce of good favor with her before, it was gone now.

"You have a lot to learn about blood. And even more about a woman's cycle. Use your implants to auto load alchemy lesson when you sleep and for the times when I knock you out during our future sparring matches. You'll be surprised what you learn."

Bandares's mind searched the implants and registered the lessons right after she said it, but he didn't immediately see how close she'd gotten till the glyphs and command images disappeared.

"Is she going to kiss me?" He wondered just before her soft, warm lips touched his.

Wanting more, he tried to kiss her back, but she broke the kiss and moved her lips to his ears, sending tingling sensations down his spine.

"Now you're getting me in trouble. Please be careful of your words. People can hear and see everything when and if it so concerns them. And blasphemy is at the top of their list."

Bandares was in shock. He knew he shouldn't have spoken ill about the sacred religion of the Empire, but he hadn't thought she'd need to pay for his words.

"Shouldn't I be punished? They're my words."

"And you're mine, Bandares. Never volunteer for punishment no matter how wrong you are. If you're wrong and nothing bad happens to you, happily stay wrong," she whispered, moving her lips in front of his once more.

After giving him a peck on the lips, she turned and walked through a force field disappearing from his view. To his right, a ramp extended downward to a silver and gold chamber filled with nude men standing in rank and file, all with distraught and weary looks on their faces.

"Tier one Bandares: Location R 21 C 6," came into his field of vision along with a directional arrow pointing to an empty space in-between the mass of men who'd already filled the chamber.

"I'm really starting not to like my implants," Bandares thought, walking hurriedly down the ramp.

Chapter IV

Blue Star

As Tara crossed through the force field, her tension eased.

"I can't believe I let him get under my skin," she thought, trying to push any sentimental thoughts about Bandares into the recesses of her mind.

"Here she is, ready to tell me what to do," she mumbled to herself, sighing as a fair-skinned woman with red hair, red lipstick, and red eye shadow appeared in front of her as she made her way through a set of round blast doors.

"I don't have time for your crap Admiral Sandreaka. What Bandares said is my responsibility. Get out of my way, I need to address them and get them boarded on your transport ship. Do your job and make sure all systems are ready and can handle the crew load instead of trying to pick holes in my troops."

"This Bandares of yours needs to be punished for his words. I've already submitted the recording to the Overseers. You should've placed him under arrest the moment those words came out of his mouth. If you don't take care of him the moment everyone's onboard, I will. I'm a Tier higher than you and-"

"Shut up. I refuse to be steam rolled by you like the other Generals unfortunate enough to be assigned to you. If you wanted Ground Assault command, you should've purposely flunked your voidship warfare assessments like everyone else."

"Are you suggesting you purposely failed your void assessments? I've sent a recording of this to the Overseers so they may analyse your tone for truth. I suggest if you have competencies in void affairs, you show them soon; that way the Overseers may be lenient if they find you've been slacking in your duties to become a well-rounded weapon of the Imperium."

"Oh, so that's what this is about. You're stepping on Generals' toes, trying to do their job because you want to show how well rounded you are. Ah, I see! You're trying to get a promotion faster than the rest. Thirty cycles and only making it to Tier five is getting under your skin huh? You're even trying to completely copy my style to make a name for yourself. Good luck with that," Tara said, instantly feeling gratified as Sandreaka's fair skin turned the same shade of red as the hair and makeup she wore.

Tara heard Sandreaka mutter something under her breath and could see she was slowly balling her fist.

"Hit me bitch, I dare you. If not, then get out of my way, they're waiting for me. If you want a promotion, do what everyone else is doing. Open your legs and mouth wide for horny Overseer whims. Oh! Wait, you're doing that already. Now, this is the last time I tell you to get out of my way before I show you how I gained my rank and reputation so fast."

"The trip to Adrasteia moon-worlds will take approximately a month and a half, and I'll be hosting four other brigades, plus yours. I assure you that the other brigade Generals are very understanding of the type of person I am, and where I stand when it comes to perfecting the Imperial way of life. I hope you and your troops have a very pleasant and safe stay aboard any void spheres I command."

The threat was clear as day that her brigade was now going to have a target painted on it, but there was nothing she could do about it. Mostly because she knew that playing nice with Sandreaka from the beginning wouldn't get her far, being that Sandreaka was the type of person who'd use every upper hand gained as a continuous stepping stone to crush a person. As Tara was considering what to say next, Sandreaka did something that let her know she hadn't lost any ground so far.

"All I see of where you stand is…out of my way. Go figure. You do have common sense," she said, walking past Sandreaka without giving her a second look.

When the blast doors closed behind her, she did a mind-synch with the ship, willing the compartment to open outwards into the chamber while simultaneously moving the location she stood outwards until it became a balcony on which she could stare down at nearly one hundred thousand men that were to be the new addition to her brigade. With their addition, the number of troops under her command would be almost an even five hundred thousand, which was the proper amount a Tier four General or Admiral should command.

Crushing the memory of what happened to her last group of new troops she'd picked up two months prior, she presented her best welcoming smile.

"New citizens of Adrasteia, I am Tier four, Ground Assault Elite General Tara. With this formality over, all of you can put a proper face to the name and image your implants have already shown you," she said before pausing to look down into the silent crowd of nude men, searching only for Bandares.

Quickly spotting him, she felt a strange sense of relief that he was still in her immediate presence. Now feeling that she'd paused for effect long enough, she spoke again with the intent to inspire people she knew were going to die in some of the most awful ways imaginable.

"How does it feel to be a citizen? Look deep inside yourself to find the answer, because that answer is the most important, substantive, and meaningful thing you can have in your life. Nurturing this feeling will be more nutritional to your soul than the love you've received from your mother," she said aloud, while telepathically sending orders to her five, Tier three Generals to begin setting further ambiance to the chamber.

Within seconds, the chamber dimmed and the music of the Empire began to play in the background. Starting with soft, yet deep beats of various drums. Following closely behind, the whisper of the wooden flutes and woodwinds. When the string instruments began to play, Tara mentally sent the order for two of her Tier three Generals to come stand a few feet behind her.

"Have you found the wonderful feeling of love and acceptance?" She asked in a hushed voice.

In response, she heard a collective murmur of acknowledgment.

"Good, that is the feeling of eternal love coming from your mother Empire, blessed by the Blood Goddesses Kali and her daughter Vajrayogini," Tara whispered, watching almost every man below cling on to her every word.

At one point, she even saw some of the men tiptoeing, causing her to almost break character.

"You idiots tiptoeing will be first to die. You have battle helmet implants, but are too dumb to turn on the advanced hearing," she thought, waiting for the music to change so that she could weave her next few words deeper into the men's souls.

Hearing the beat pick up ever so slightly, she mentally ordered the two, Tier three Generals who'd come behind her to cast an alchemic spell on the rock floor beneath the men—so that it'd lift and float just below the balcony.

"Now that all of you feel enveloped by the love of Adrasteia, all of you can rest assured you'll never become unloved by her. After all, the name Adrasteia means 'inescapable.' Which means, we're all wrapped in inescapable love. Take another moment to let that sink in," she said as softly as she could, watching the men below her becoming a mass of hypnotised souls.

"Out of the crowd, I can only see nine not falling for it. I wish Bandares wouldn't be so obvious about it. Please stop looking around at the brainwashed idiots, play along like the rest. No! Don't poke him Bandares. You'll be the death of me!" She thought, wanting to burst out laughing.

"He's both frustrating and intriguing. I can't really put a finger on the type of person he is. All I know so far is that he's not inherently narcissistic and cold blooded, which is a rare trait in this Empire for certain," she thought sucking in a deep breath, ensuring she repressed any reaming feelings of amusement.

As she stilled herself, the floor in which the men stood began to glow with intricate sacred geometric patterns in the form of electric trace lines.

"A show of force to all those who've never seen the power of body alchemy used upon inanimate, non-mechanical structures such as the floor you stand upon. Behold a true testament to the power you'll be able to gain, embraced by the inescapable love of your mother Empire!" She exclaimed, making sure she made eye contact with Bandares, hoping he'd understand that the religious and alchemical practice of ingesting a woman's cycle was something he should take very seriously.

With their eyes locked, she could already tell he no longer doubted the power of body alchemy. This gave her reassurance that he'd do as she'd asked him in terms of studying alchemy further. Breaking eye contact with him, she watched the floor as it lifted almost directly level with her balcony.

"It's time we head off to do the bidding of our beloved Empress Dakini. Rest assured, all of you will play a vital role, for all of you aid to the power of her conviction!" Tara said, stepping off the makeshift balcony onto the perfectly removed, half-inch thick rock surface.

"I wonder how long this hypnosis will last. Three days? Less if they start to mingle with all the others from my command or even worse with the other brigades," she thought as she looked down the rows and columns of mindless, grinning faces.

Turning around, she took control of the floating platform and proceeded to bring it into the opening of the voidship. Laying the platform down into the large open space, she simply walked away sending her five, Tier three Generals mental messages, letting them know she trusted them to take care of getting the men settled.

"That was impressive, I recorded this event and requested you undergo an audit in which Overseers evaluate your proficiency in alchemy. It's already been approved. I also requested that I'd be the evaluator of your voidship and void knowledge capabilities. This has also been approved. I'm sending you the authentication now," Sandreaka said as Tara made it out of the large bay into the passageway leading to her chamber.

Tara barely had enough time to even see who was talking. After realising who it was and understanding what she'd just heard, her mind shifted gears from worry over her new troops, to a dark place, where she was almost willing to kill Sandreaka and throw her life away.

"She must be giving her body out like a treat to these Overseers. I wonder how many are aboard her main ship or how many are here on this transport ship?" She wondered, checking the roster for Overseers and finding none.

"Annoying, whenever they pretend they're not sleuthing about, I can rest assured they are. Question is, why are they watching so close?" She pondered, turning to look at Sandreaka.

"You're very beautiful, I'd want a piece of you myself if your kunuss wasn't infected with every Venusian disease in the known universe. Must smell terrible…I even hear you shower alone? I can't help but question your state of mind as an Admiral. One who doesn't upkeep one's mind, body, and spirit enough to keep her legs closed to those of higher powers, surely cannot keep all that's under her jurisdiction in order."

"How dare you!" Sandreaka growled, making Tara want to dig in more.

"Overseers must not be able to see or smell? Or maybe because they're miserable and sick, they just don't care who they hurt. Since I can clearly see you're unable to even maintain yourself, you'll definitely not be able to maintain me. By the way, there's something on your lip, you should go find out which strain it is.

FYI, there's a new strain that makes it to the brain pretty fast. Oh, and I documented your physical health and sent it to the Overseers, requesting an audit of your health and mindset, starting with a pap test. It's already been approved. I am sending you the authentication now," Tara said, feeling her heart pounding in her chest as she tried to make her lie a reality.

Tara only knew one Overseer that she could call in a favor or two from, but she hated having to use a favor on something she'd normally consider trivial. Worrying her even more was getting caught in her bluff. Sending a peer-check request was so out of her character, she doubted she'd even receive a response from said Overseer, let alone a yes.

"You wouldn't... you're bluffing," Sandreaka chocked out, just before folding her lip over the blister that appeared to be growing with every second that passed.

"Damn my luck! She's not going to respond is she?" Tara assumed just as an incoming authentication appeared in her mind.

"No bluff, you should've seen the authentication by now. Unless, you're having trouble with your implants? If that's the case, I'll augment my peer check request to that of full physical," Tara said, forwarding the authentication now that she'd triple checked it for time stamps.

"I have it, I have it!" Sandreaka blurted out.

"Good, I'll call you when I am ready. As usual for a pap test, I ask that you do not hygiene or alter the natural state or scents of your body," Tara said, walking away as calmly as she could.

As she rounded the bend in the honeycomb-shaped passageway, she almost took off running. Behind her, she could already hear Sandreaka shrieking and cursing her name and thought, *"that's what you get when you play too much politics."*

The thought didn't make her feel any better, and Tara couldn't help but feel dirty about the way she'd just handled Sandreaka. However, her alternative choice of killing her ten ways wouldn't have been in her best interest of self-preservation. Stopping just shy of entering her chamber, she realised she was trembling.

"That kind of fighting isn't for me," she mumbled to herself, clinching her fist.

"**All hands prepare for launch. All Ground Assault personnel are ordered into stasis until otherwise noted.**"

"What! I cannot believe it! How is this possible? No one travels in stasis for a month and a half trip. How's she doing this? All this, just to get out of it, right bitch? I promise I will!-" Tara grit her teeth not wanting to finish her threat, knowing that everything she said and did was being watched by the hundreds of live image feeds integrated inside the voidship bulkheads.

"Time till launch. Ten minutes."

"Rahh!" Tara screamed, punching the blast door of her chamber with her armored fist as she opened a channel to Sandreaka.

"You know as well as I, the people that just came aboard need more implants and time to adjust to them before drop! What are you doing? Stop playing with people's lives because of your stupid pride!" She screamed, quivering in anger.

"Some peoples' pride are the foundation of their entire life. So when you try to crush it, don't be surprised the lengths they go to try and protect it. Hindering your unit's function hinders my beloved Empire's goals. I'd never do anything to obstruct the Blood Empress's vision of all solar systems and all planets unified under Adrasteia's inescapable rule. I'll have all of you awoken two weeks before we arrive in Adrasteia binary. That'll give you three days to have all of them undergo their surgeries and the remainder of the days to adjust and train before we are scheduled to reach our target.

I've cleared this with the Overseers and your Tier five General as well as my Tier six Admiral. Sending you authentication now. I hope you sleep very well, Blue Star," Sandreaka replied in a calm practiced voice, making Tara feel butterflies in her stomach as she thought of all the horrible things that could go wrong while she along with her brigade were in stasis.

"There's got to be something I can do! I've got to stop this!" She thought, sensing people behind her.

Turning around, she saw four people covered in the sleek, dark grey body armor that voidship personnel favored.

"What do you four want? Don't you have duties to carry out?" She asked bitterly.

"We were sent here to aid you into your stasis pod," a woman replied.

Behind them, she saw four more people appear, each one coming from the other four brigades assigned to Sandreaka's voidship.

"Launch order clarification: Only "Blue Star" Brigade will be going into stasis. Launch in six minutes."

Behind those four, a line started to form four-wide in the passageway in front of her chamber, with various men and women from the other brigades as well as voidship personnel. Tears began to run down her face as she heard some of the people laugh, talking openly about the mean and disgusting things they planned to do to her.

"All of you are evil," she whispered, turning around and walking through the blast door into her chamber.

Moving swiftly to the stasis pod, she took hold of it and moved it till it was just a few feet shy from the entrance. Looking back, she saw the line getting longer. Sucking in her breath to hold back more tears, she turned around and willed her armor to fold and retract into her body, then bent over and laid on top of the composite, crystalline surface of the pod.

"The first of you ...or all of you come," she forced herself to say, feeling her legs quiver as many of the crowd rushed into her chamber.

"Direct image to Admiral Sandreaka," she commanded.

"Oh! I see you-" Sandreaka trailed off, letting Tara know her insane plan would most likely work.

"I choose to be totally awake for this. Punish me how see fit for breaking your orders. But I figured you'd like to watch," she said, shuttering as she felt hands gripping her waist and the warmth of a body along her legs and thighs.

Through her tears, Tara watched Sandreaka look into her eyes as a woman began to thrust her fingers inside her. At first Sandreaka kept a solid remorseless face, but after the first few minutes in which at least ten women and four men had their way with her, Sandreaka turned her head. Then as the voidship began to lift, Sandreaka cut the imager.

"Blue Star brigade will return to active passenger status. All brigades muster with unit commanders on respective brigade levels effective immediately. All voidship personnel not at duty stations must return at once. This order will not be repeated, and those who do not follow will be punished without recourse," Tara heard from the PA, just as someone released inside her.

"Move out of her quickly, I want to give Blue Star one last parting gift," Tara heard a woman say, picking up the scent of putrid kunuss, as the man slipped out of her.

"Take this bitch," the woman said, jamming her fingers coated with infected kunuss fluid inside of her.

I'll kill all of you. I promise on my soul, I'll kill all of you, Tara thought, collecting facial images from her chamber and from the passageway.

"I'd like to give you something as well," Tara whispered, closing her eyes as she concentrated on the chakra point inside her kunuss.

"What'd you say, you annoying goody, goody bitch?" The woman replied, removing her fingers just before appearing in front of her face.

Tara channeled even more energy into her womb and collected all the kunuss and kudock fluid harboring thousands, if not millions, of Venusian causing pathogens, then triggered her cycle. With her blood and ethereal energy merging in her kunuss, she formed an entanglement point connecting herself with everyone who'd been inside her or had even touched her for a moment.

"I'll make your deaths drag out for at least a week or two," she whispered, sending the potent mix of bacteria, virus and fungi directly into the people's bodies.

"I'll kill the ones who hadn't had a chance to touch me with a more personal approach," she decided, smiling at the woman as she asked "can you see it yet? The blue stars forming in your vision?"

"No, you crazy bitch. What are you talking about? Are you chanting your name? I'm happy we broke you. I hope you stay broken. Keep chanting your name for all to see that you're a nobody, just like us."

"Blue star, Blue star," Tara whispered over and over sarcastically in a robotic voice.

"We all hate people like you. You think you're better than us, climbing in Tiers when others stay at Tier one and two their entire lives… like me."

Hearing the woman's words made Tara smile.

"Well you don't have to worry much longer about that. When you see the blue stars, they've entered your brain," she whispered, pushing herself off of the crystalline pod.

Not bothering to listen to the woman's retort or call out her armor, she turned and walked out of her chamber, pushing and shoving people still clogged in the passageway who were all to selfish to create a traffic flow. As per usual, everyone was preferring to walk whichever way they thought best to get to their mustering location, believing everyone else should move out the way for them.

Chapter V

How is this censored?

AS THE SHOCK WAVE TRAVELED through Wa'raydon, flame-retardant tree sap filled the entire family unit within a hundredth of a second. A hundredth of a second later, Wa'raydon watched thick leaves and vines covering his parents, the infants, his voidship, the balcony entrance, and finally himself.

Wa'raydon knew everything happened just in the nick of time because he felt the pressure and intense heat of the main shock wave slam against his building even after being wrapped in the thick cocoon.

"Is it over?" He wondered, feeling the pressure and heat die down.

Almost instantly after the thought crossed his mind, tree sap filled the rest of his cocoon, completely submerging him. Explosions followed immediately after, and this time, it felt as though they were right on top of his building. At one point, a piece of his cocoon ruptured, allowing an intense wave of heat and pressure to enter, searing through the sap and grazing his outer bicep.

"I want out of here! I want to see if everyone is alright!" He kept thinking to himself, trying to flex his body as tiny vines pressed into his nose, lungs, and damaged bicep.

When he was totally immobilised, he felt the tree sap begin to vibrate on his skin.

"What's this vibration? Is there another attack happening further away?"

"Status: Healed," flashed across his inner vision.

"Trace source of signal," he commanded to his implants, seeing that the signal registered as undefinable.

"Source untraceable," his implants replied, showing him all the planetary networks, indicating which were operational and which were not.

"What kind of signal was that?" He wondered, changing his implants

setting from auto search to manual.

Pressing his consciousness into the building's computer network, he saw odd signals embedded in the network code that would sporadically appear and disappear.

"Embedded organic code. But, it doesn't appear to be like the organic code from the tree. G'o's signal is always clean, almost mechanical. This code looks a lot different, but maybe…"

"G'o, is that a different form of your organic code running through the network? And can you show me the status of my family?" He asked the tree telepathically.

At his request, images of his family appeared in his mind as well as images of the absolute carnage outside. As Wa'raydon read the health status of his family, he felt the cocoon unwrapping around him. Just before the last portion pulled away, he saw and felt a group of vines pressing into both his navel and back of his neck.

"Ow! What gives?" He grunted, turning his head to the left to peer into the love-making chamber before looking back towards the kitchen.

From the stats G'o had shown him, his mother had taken the most damage during the attack, but had also been healed.

"Hey, how is everyone?" He called out, wanting to hear if they were okay from their own mouths as he watched the cocoons unwrapping around them.

Instead of answering verbally, Re'meka and Adenetta ran and smashed into him, hugging him, then pushing him out of the way as they ran full speed towards the cocoons that held the infants, which had by that time unwrapped into leaf-like cradles. Wa'raydon would've done the same, but the pain in his stomach and neck where the vines had entered his body was intensifying.

"Son, are you okay? You're bleeding," his father said, hugging his mother, who was moving shakenly to the leaf cradles.

After his father mentioned he was bleeding, Re'meka, Adenetta, and his mother all stopped and stared at him with a mix of horrified looks on their faces.

"This is…this is…" Wa'raydon felt the vines moving within his body, traveling to his brain through his intestine and up along his spinal cord.

As the vines grew, the pain slowly eased. And when the sensation of their growth ended, an extremely clear mental image display appeared in his mind's eye, replacing the mental image display his implants had always provided.

"Organic signals classified: Multiple sentient beings."

"G'o, that's vague. Multiple sentient beings what?"

"Son?"

"It's okay, I umm, think G'o merged a piece of itself in me," he said, taking his first pain free steps towards his family.

"G'o…care to explain why?" He asked telepathically, annoyed and slightly afraid the tree had taken it upon itself to connect with his body on such an intimate level.

Its response, "Immanent danger," didn't make him feel any more secure.

"Tell us what your briefing was about," Re'meka said angrily, with tears running down her cheeks.

"I have an idea of what it was about," his mother said standing up, calling body armor out of her flesh.

"Mom?" Wa'raydon asked in surprise, never seeing his mother in armor in his forty cycles of life.

"Did I raise an Admiral for a son, or a gawker? Get on your coms and call your upper chain of command. Find out how Adrasteia is already at our throats!" His mother screamed, causing all of the infants to cry.

"Yes mother," Wa'raydon said, still in shock at the sight of his mother as he transmitted signals to both Admiral Botatu and to his voidship still berthed inside of Botatu's.

As he transmitted, he watched Adenetta and his father call up real-time holo-images of the planet, just in time to see hundreds of spherical voidships bearing the colors and insignia of his world, hurtling towards the planet's Capitol which lay in the northern hemisphere, almost half the distance away from them.

"Our planet already seems lost," Re'meka gasped, adding to the pure horror already gripping him as he watched one voidship after another slam upon the shields of the Capitol.

"The people aboard those ships!" Wa'raydon choked out as he received weak distress signals from the crews onboard his ship and Admiral Botatu's.

"They're trapped aboard! The ships have been hacked!" He finally managed to say.

"How many of yours are trapped sweetie? I'm sure today isn't the day you choose to be stringent on crew leave," his mother said with a straight tone, giving him a look that made him feel proud of himself, yet somehow still like a child.

"I sent most to the surface the moment I got permission. My voidship is minimally manned with a crew of only fifteen thousand, in which I left a Tier three in charge. Two hundred and fifty eight thousand have mustered directly under me.

One hundred sixty-two thousand are confirmed dead from the bombardment, in which I lost four of my Tier three Admirals and more than half of my Tier two squad leaders. I'm waiting for news from the rest now," Wa'raydon whispered, cringing as choppy, yet high quality images from inside both his ship and Admiral Botatu's played out inside his head, showing both crews trying to regain control of their ships.

"Son, how clearly can you see the situation within the ships?" His father asked in tone that gave Wa'raydon the feeling his father had a better idea of what's going on than he was letting on.

"I can see into my own ship and Admiral Botatu's. From my ship, I can receive wisp of audio message from my crew and the ship's network, but nothing coherent. From Admiral Botatu's void ship, I'm only receiving silent image feeds. And no matter how hard I try to push my way through the network, I still hear nothing. Nor can I send a message to either ship. And…"

"And?" His father pressed.

"Well, the other thing that's really bothering me is that I can't find Admiral Botatu, either by video feed or by beacon. As a matter of fact, his beacon is sporadically showing up all over our ships. Why do you ask dad, what are you thinking?"

"He's thinking you won't' like what he's thinking. G'o, I give you permission to merge with my newborns… Ladies."

"Mom?"

"Son, now is not the time for this talk."

"G'o. I give you permission as well," Re'meka said, grabbing hold of Adenetta's hand as Adenetta said, "I the same."

Wa'raydon looked into the leaf cradles and watched tiny vines enter the infant's stomach and neck.

"Hey? What's going on?" He asked, feeling his blood begin to boil.

"Bid your crew farewell," his mother replied, and when he looked up from the infants, he could see the imager was now focused on Admiral Botatu's voidship coming into atmosphere.

Barreling down at high speed, it opened fire in every direction. From the holo-imager and from the signals he was receiving from inside both voidships, he witnessed his voidship launch out of its holding bay like a projectile to slam upon the Capitol's shields just a mere second before Botatu's.

"RAH!" He screamed in anger as every image coming from inside the two voidships ceased, leaving him staring numbly at the shimmering shield, now showing signs it was about to fail.

"I wasn't even able to say goodbye! Something was blocking me from sending anything the entire time!" He bellowed, stealing a guilty glance at the infants, worried his outburst would send them into another crying fit, only to find that they were sound asleep, which made him realise that they'd actually stopped crying the moment the vines had entered their bodies.

"I count thirty-six more voidships still on course for the Capitol. Whoever's controlling them isn't going to want the shields to have a chance to recover, so I'm betting they'll do a full weapons launch targeting only the Capitol this time as opposed to our unshielded cities and farmlands," Adenetta said, bringing up an imager that played out the entire attack from the moment it began.

"All the ships that are hacked are from my fleet. See the insignia. Our flotilla was four hundred sixty three strong, consisting of mostly Tier four and below voidships. Remember when I left, what I said about my deployment?"

"Yes son, they wanted younger Admirals to go on longer deployments like how it used to be. I think the idea was to keep your generation from becoming complacent. And I agreed with that idea, even though I hated seeing you gone for so long. But I see your Fleet Admiral had something else in mind. How close of a pass did you make near any of the two thousand entanglement points leading to planet Adrasteia? And did you see or hear any rumors about someone from your armada going to meet anyone from the Heka moon-worlds?" His mother asked, sounding pensive.

"Hold on mom, I'm having my surviving crew muster here. I told them to bring anything they can fly," he said as he instructed his troops to live stream directly to him so that he may gain a greater scope of the damage brought upon the planet.

"I want my family to see too," he thought as he called up two holo-imagers.

"Here's a cluster stream of real-time info from my people. And here's an imager of my memories during my deployment. I spent a lot of time synced with the ship. It's possible I collected pieces of info that can help us."

Saying that, Wa'raydon remembered what Admiral Botatu said about the mathematical equations.

"Use small pieces to see the larger one," he whispered to himself.

"Son?" His father said.

"Nothing. So, the only entanglement point linking to that damned planet we came close to was almost out of the binary system. And, I remember the blockade got real agitated as we started moving towards it, so we ended up stopping around twenty light minutes away," Wa'raydon said as he expanded the holographic images wider so that everyone could see the data.

"She is making her final run on the Capitol," his father said, sounding exhausted, bringing Wa'raydon's attention back to the imager showing the last of the hijacked ships hurtling towards the Capitol.

As Adenetta had predicted, the ships hadn't fired until they were perfectly aligned with the Capitol. Now that they were, every ship simultaneously fired powerful lasers and launched every sort of explosive kinetic projectile in their arsenal.

"She," Wa'raydon said, more as a statement than a question, knowing that only Tier twelve Admirals or above had the ability to take over so many ships at the same time.

"Why would Admiral Mezmeca do this? It makes no sense to help Adrasteia. None at all," he kept thinking, flinching as he watched the weapons crash against the shields.

"The Capitol's shields are failing. I wonder how many were able to make it to the shelter ships underground," his father said, shaking his head sadly.

"At least they have city shields. Where were ours? The government has been promising us for cycles that they'd install them. That was their reason for raising taxes. Where'd they spend all those credits? Oh, I know. It was on themselves. All for what? All to make themselves the main target and receive the heaviest attacks," Adenetta said bitterly as a bright blue-white flash indicated to Wa'raydon and everyone else that the shields had finally failed.

The next few flashes he saw sent complex emotions between rage and numbness coursing through his body.

"Two and a half billion people, just gone," he muttered, incapable of absorbing the vast number of people that'd turned to ashes in mere seconds.

"We're next. Armour up everyone, things are going to get a lot worse," his father said, causing bile to rise in Wa'raydon throat.

"And how do you know? What in the seven lives is going on? All of you are keeping something from me. And I'm not okay with what just happened with the children. As their father, I should have say in what goes inside my children," he said, fixing his two mates scalding glares.

"We didn't mean to exclude you-"

"You did exclude me! Yes, I see the difference."

"Wa'raydon, now is not the time," his father said, raising his arms.

Trace lines of vines and roots started running through his father's flesh, making Wa'raydon's skin crawl.

"Dad, your skin?" He said as he tried to swallow down the bile that persisted to rise in his throat no matter how many times he swallowed.

"Trust me son. It's time to armor-up."

Right after his father said that, an explosion felt like it went off directly underneath their family unit.

"I see your point," he mumbled, commanding his armor to extend out of his body.

"WOW! What is this?" He asked in a hushed startled voice, unprepared for what he saw on himself.

No one replied, but none seem surprised either.

"My implants feel strange. What is this?" He asked again, this time more forcefully as he stared at his body armor which was now a mixture of green, brown, and blue hues, vice the normal color of his armor that resembled the metal Orichalcum.

"Organic metal son. Don't worry, it won't hurt you," his mother said calmly.

"What in the seven lives is going on? Tell me now! The closest of my troops can't even make the final few miles of the journey here. As all of you can see, they're taking fire from the ground as well as from other void commands! How does a civil war break out, yet mother blurts out that Adrasteia is at our throats!?" He shouted, feeling betrayed by his families tight-lip behaviour.

Turning towards his mother, he could see she was gazing at the infants in the leaf cradle with a solemn face that almost made him feel guilty for yelling. He could also see that her armor had changed drastically from when she'd first summoned it out of her body and that it now resembled his own and everyone else's. Noticing his glare, his mother took a deep breath and opened her mouth, but before she could say a word, a deep powerful horn blared with a vibration so intense it made his lungs rattle.

Coughing, he tilted his head and commanded his new helmet

interface to buffer the sound as it dug into his inner ear while thinking, *"am I the only one feeling this?,"* noticing that his entire family appeared totally calm.

"Why are they staring straight ahead like that? It looks like they're possessed," he started to think, becoming nervous.

"People of Ah Tabai, it's time to fight back our oppressors once more," Wa'raydon heard a raspy female voice announce from the holo-imager showing the destruction of the Capitol.

One by one, all the holo-imagers he and his family had summoned began to close, until all that remained was the one in which the female voice had come from. Slowly the image of the burning, gutted Capitol faded, revealing a dark smoke like silhouette of a female.

"For those of you who remember when we first came to this moon-world, you know that we came here for peace. The Blood Empress of Adrasteia granted us this moon-world, promising no more bloodshed and war as a reward for the hundreds of cycles of loyal service we'd given her. She'd even went so far as to kneel in front of us all, swearing upon her vulgar Goddesses that she'd never ask us to join her warrior ranks again.

Yet ten cycles later, she'd come calling us back to another pointless and violent war. And when we refused to go, we were attacked with a Tier one siege that left twenty-four billion dead! Elven billion of our children kidnaped and enslaved! All the while, leaving the rest of us to die, slow miserable deaths on the surface of this planet, which they had purposely stripped bare of water and all other substantive forms of life."

"Umm, this wasn't taught to me in history class," Wa'raydon said in a low exasperated tone, still keeping an eye on his troops live feed using his mind's eye - noticing that ever since the woman had come on the holo-imager, they were taking on heavier amounts of fire.

"At this rate, none of them are going to make it here. I have to try and save as many as I can, no matter what the risk is to my own chakra system," he decided, channeling as much body energy as he could muster into his peoples' downed or severely damaged, yet still flying vessels.

Once his body energy was integrated within the vessels, he focused on repairing them back to a self-substantive level in which they'd be able to administer aid to the injured or dying crew. Noticing that the enemy continued to fire into his troop ships even after they were down, he decided it was worth the risk to remotely fly even the most damaged of them in hopes he could bring them to safety.

"All hands: Don't get caught up in dogfights that could divide you. Regrouping here is top priority!" He sent telepathically, seeing that his overeager pilots were getting picked off faster than the rest.

"We, however, persevered! And this is thanks to the hundreds of sentient beings that also consider this world their home. Without them returning after Adrasteia's Tier one siege, we wouldn't have been able to rebuild and push the Adrasteian's away from our moon-world and all the others!"

"Are you kidding me? So our moon-world was the catalyst of all the other moon-worlds rebelling against the Adrasteia Empire?" Wa'raydon screamed, shaking his head in disgust.

"We censored much of our history from the children born after we gained our freedom, in hopes they'd never need to witness the nightmare we lived through. We thought that doctored-warnings and half-truths would be enough to keep them aware of the danger without living in paranoia as we have for so many cycles.

But as we can see now, it was the wrong decision. For all of you who were alive during my time, show our children the monsters we're up against and show them the monsters we used to be! Because becoming monsters again...is the only thing that'll save us now!"

The imager cut and dissolved, leaving all of them facing a dark green leaf wall, in which Wa'raydon felt he could almost still see the dark slender silhouette of the woman whose eyes had flashed bright green at the closing of her speech.

"Son?" His father said softly.

"Yes, I'm just thinking. You know, Admiral Botatu told me to watch the uncensored version of Adrasteia's Tier one sieges against the R'yu, Yin't and Yin'n systems. At the time, I thought it was odd he said that. Because, when we first joined the Void fleet, we all watched the first day siege of planet R'yu. There was enough gore, dust, and ash in the documentary to last me all seven life times. But now I realize that uncensored means without lies spliced in," Wa'raydon said, turning to look his parents in the eyes.

"Botatu knew me just as well as the two of you. He knew I'd bring it up to you instead of just trying to find the documentaries on my own. Now, I'm left wondering how much was edited because as brutal as that documentary was, it seemed pretty normal in terms of warfare. Even I've taken out thousands of Void pirates with zero recourse. So what do the Adrasteian's do that makes them so different when it comes to killing?" He asked, feeling his back muscles tighten in reflexive aggravation.

"Well for one thing they-"

A series of explosions interrupted his mother and caused the entire building to sway. At the same time, he started to see the first of his troops closing in on his location from their live feed.

"Set this pattern and fire at any identifiable enemies," Wa'raydon commanded, sending a mental picture of a vortex surrounding his mega building.

"Hostiles inside of your building Admiral?" Many of his troops asked.

"All single-person vessels link up to form ten-person spheres. After you group up, the five with the most ground combat experience will act as boarding party to comb through the building. Each pilot will have a single-mind link with one of the boarding party members.

As you team members fall in combat, relink accordingly. I'm also assigning one person to act as a hub for every fifty mind-links, and that hub person will connect to me. Assignments complete, I'll be airborne shortly," Wa'raydon replied telepathically.

"My troops are here, I have them forming a fence around the building as well as Ground Assault teams to comb through it. There's still the problem that I've yet to figure out who the enemy are.

Since that doesn't seem to be a problem for the enemy, who shots with reckless abandon, I told my troops to kill anyone who makes a move against them. Speaking of which, I can't figure out why anyone would side with Adrasteia if they're so terrible," he said, making his way to the thick leaf still covering the balcony along with his voidship.

"Are you going out there?" Re'meka asked, moving towards him.

"What kind of Admiral doesn't fly with his people? Of course I am."

"At least stay with us till we get the children down below and into the shelter ships," Adenetta chimed in.

"Stop bluffing, Adenetta. If you felt it was safe to go down, you'd have dragged all of us down there yourself. I feel the same as you, there might be those who sympathise with Adrasteia waiting in the shelter ships, ready to blow them up."

"That already happened son, remember those explosions under our feet just a few moments ago?" His mother said in a matter of fact tone that somehow got on his last nerve.

"I didn't see this indicated on the building network," he replied defensively, checking the status of the shelter ships.

"It says they're all operational. So, what are you trying to say mom?"

"The entire building network, backup, and subsystems are

destroyed. The network you see is operated by the enemy, hoping people will still try to make their way down there. It's a deathtrap for all who aren't connected to G'o. You would've known when they were destroyed as well, but I had asked G'o not to show you yet. Speaking of which, G'o has been acting as our main network, which is the only reason why we're still able to use the holo-imagers."

"This whole situation is insane! Wouldn't G'o help others like he's helping us? And why are you taking it upon yourself to keep things from me?"

"I can't speak for G'o in terms of who it'll help or who it wouldn't. I do know G'o is way past half way into the next life," his mother said, giving him a look he dubbed as her 'mood check' look.

"Stop staring at me like that. I can handle my emotions."

"I know you, and earlier you weren't ready to hear that type of bad news about the shelter ships or about G'o," his mother said, calling forth an almost translucent trident.

"Why do you say that? Tell me mom, why wouldn't I've been able to handle it before?" He retorted quickly.

"My gut feeling is the only answer I have for you. And the reasoning behind my gut feeling is a parent thing. It's the reason why your father and I never told you or your older siblings the truth. Why we pretended we knew nothing about the uncensored documentaries of Adrasteia's Tier one sieges.

We wanted to protect all of you, to keep all of you happy, or as happy as we could. Even after all of that protecting, every single one of your older brothers and sisters found a way into their second life before their parents. So right now, I'd be satisfied with keeping you level headed so that you don't make a silly mistake and end up joining them. This is how parents always think. Look at your children sleeping through this chaos. When they grow older, do you want them to remember times like this? That they lived through a nightmare?"

"No," he replied softly, understanding his mother's words.

"I'm glad you see it my way. I also need you to understand that under no circumstance are you to go out there and fly with your troops unless I say otherwise, which I highly doubt I will. And if you take one more step towards your void sphere, my trident will go through one of your feet."

"Don't tell me!"

Wa'raydon didn't see the trident move from her hand before he felt something wrong with his left foot.

"Ah!" He screamed, seeing the trident protruding from his foot.

Looking around, he could see Re'meka and Adenetta moving between his mother and the leaf cradles looking just as bewildered. His father however looked totally calm.

"Son, what else did Admiral Botatu say to you?" His father asked, locking eyes with him.

"He just said to study the uncensored Tier one sieges."

"And?" His father said moving closer.

"Why would you hurt your son!?" Adenetta shouted.

"G'o's spore will heal him when the trident is removed. Calm down," his mother replied causally, not taking her eyes off him to address the blade forming in Adenetta's hand.

"Botatu told me not to talk about the equations. And if anyone asked, to say it was normal math in my head...but they're my parents," Wa'raydon thought.

"That's all you have to say on this matter?" His father said as he placed his hand on the trident.

"Yes! That's it!" Wa'raydon replied, deciding to keep the secret.

"Okay, it just seems odd. We know you do a lot of math in your head, but when you first arrived your brainwaves were giving off something odd."

"Brain waves?" Wa'raydon asked as he mentally checked the settings of his implants, reviewing the logs to see what emotion-based thoughts his implants had sent to his family members.

"All normal thoughts - Fear, anxiety, anger, small ponderings, and all the other things I choose to share. And I know I made sure I gave myself a two minute clear my mind period to keep the equations far away from my thoughts as I landed. So there's no way he should've picked up any of my brainwaves. Or anything from my implants," he thought frantically.

"I said what I meant," his father said, yanking the trident out of his foot, and before he could even scream, his foot felt normal again.

"Learn to keep your brainwaves under tighter wraps, my son. Brain waves are one of the most powerful things humans possess. But it's also a person's biggest weakness, especially when their thoughts are used against them. The Adrasteia Empire has a unit just for this purpose. They're called the Hakini, which is a nice way to say 'Mind-stealers'," his father said kneeling down, resting a hand on his left foot while still maintaining eye contact with him.

"A unit of people who can literally steal your mind...going after the persons brain waves?" Wa'raydon asked, trying to imagine how the process worked, hoping if he ever encountered such people, he could do something about it.

"Yes son. Exactly so. And I know better than most how powerful this unit is, because a long time ago, I was a part of that unit," his father said, sounding regretful.

"I…dad, what are you doing to me? I feel-" Wa'raydon felt heat running into his left foot, then up the left side of his body.

When the sensation reached the base of his neck, a very faint image of Admiral Botatu connected to hundreds if not thousands of wires and cables appeared in his mind. Next to Botatu, he could see Mezmeca sitting nude with three orbs of blood floating in front of her. In the middle of each orb of blood, thousands of translucent filaments extend out, plugging into both the voidship and into various parts of Botatu's body.

"Remember you said you could see Admiral Botatu's beacon of all over your voidships and his. And remember your mother told you, you wouldn't like what you were going to hear. Well, now you can see why his signal showed up everywhere. Right now, I'm able to capture some of his brainwaves. As you can see, he's aboard a small two person voidship with your former fleet Admiral Mezmeca. Sorry son, but your mentor is also responsible for hijacking the voidships of your armada."

"No way!" Wa'raydon exclaimed as the image of his long time mentor grew clearer and stronger in his mind's eye.

Chapter VI

Upgrade

BANDARES AWOKE CONFUSED, WITH drool running from the corners of his mouth and an odd numb sensation in his body from his neck down. When he tried to move, he found only his head and neck responding. And he dared not open his eyes fully, because every time he tried, the light of the chamber seemed to pierce into the back of his skull. The only thing he could hear was ringing and a low hum. Then when he tried to call out for help, he found his tongue was totally unresponsive.

"What's wrong with me? Where am I? Why can't I remember how I got here?" He thought, activating his implants, searching for the last moments he remembered.

Images formed in his mind's eye in which he could see himself standing in the row and column he'd been assigned to. After a few seconds, he saw himself filing into an immense circular elevator capable of accommodating everyone in his row with room to spare. As the elevator began to move, the order for his brigade to go into stasis had come.

After the order, the elevator stopped and the bulkhead of the voidship surrounding the elevator began to spin. As the bulkhead spun, blast doors opened while instructions appeared in his head guiding him when and where to walk. A few short minutes later, he entered a chamber filled with two hundred stasis pods. Standing next to each pod were men and women in various battle armor, which his implants annotated were from the various brigades assigned to the voidship. His memory focused longest on their evil grins as he stepped into the pod before his memory went blank.

"I take it I'm in this current state because of them," Bandares supposed, feeling a mix of emotions spanning from relief that he was still alive, to fear that he may be a paraplegic forever.

"Keep trying to move your body. Keep trying to open your eyes," he encouraged himself, noticing that he was regaining feeling in his tongue as the smell of antiseptics registered in his mind.

Shortly afterwards, he was able to keep his eyes open fully, and as his vision unclouded, he could make out the color blue. The next thing he recognised was the voice speaking, but his ears were still ringing, making it hard to understand exactly what she was saying.

"Wha-?" He mumbled awkwardly trying to make his tongue to move correctly.

Blinking away the last of the blurriness, Bandares instantly wished he hadn't.

"Ga...get me out of here," he stuttered, catching the first glimpse of his mutilated body which was being suspended within a levitation field.

Bandares shock wasn't only due to the state he saw himself in. Directly across from him, he could see the mutilated body of Yon'tu hovering in a levitation field as well. Staring at Yon'tu's open stomach for longer than he should've, he felt an urge to throw-up. However, the sensation ended as a laser activated, slicing into his own stomach, first horizontally then vertically.

"Decompression protection units need to be embedded in your stomach, intestinal tract, all of your major blood vessels, heart, lungs, oh...and in your entire face. If you were to get sucked out into the void during an attack, the first places that'd rupture would be your sinus passageways, your anus, and the one men never think about, your kudock.

The bladder sometimes even tears away and tries to come out through the hole. Oh! Or sometimes, the piss comes rushing out and then freezes. But most are dead by then. You know, you don't instantly freeze...well you do in deep void, but not near a planet where it's more likely for people like us to get sucked out."

"Tara? Why am I awake for this? Why am I being made to watch this? Just put me back to sleep!" Bandares screamed, feeling his tongue working properly again.

"No can do right now. You've already been out for a day and a half and everything we could do while you were asleep, we've done already. The next few hours are the preliminary test of your new implants. This is when your nerve-to-brain connections, along with the brain waves you emit when you're awake are tracked so that adjustments can be made on your implants."

"But."

"No but, you need to be awake. This is the only way to make sure your implants work seamlessly with both your body and your mind. Trust me, you don't want to skip this step. The other test after this are far worse."

Bandares didn't know what to say, but every fiber in his being wished he could argue otherwise. Seeing his body in its current state made him feel paranoid that something could go horribly wrong if he merely looked at himself for too long. Locking eyes with Tara, he tried to give her a reassuring smile, letting her knew he understood that he needed to be awake. Nonetheless, he was certain the smile came out looking like a confused frown when Tara snorted and began to laugh.

"Your face just now. Ah, I don't think I'll ever see something like that again, even in my remaining lives. Unless, you can make it for me again?"

Bandares opted to stare at her blankly, not feeling amused at his situation whatsoever.

"Yhea, that's a no. Anyways, you don't actually get sucked out into the void. Well, you do sometimes, depending on the circumstance. Either way, after an attack on a voidship, many people end up out in the void.

So you're probably thinking how's that possible if the voidship actually implodes where struck due to the safety measures that try to decompress the chamber after a hull breach? Let's see if you're smart, what's the flaw in our safety systems that still allows large amounts of people to end up in the void after a hull breach?"

Bandares could barely focus on the question. He'd caught a glimpse of his reflection on one of the thicker portions of the suspension beam where he could see his brain with thousands, if not more, tiny needles protruding from it.

"Hey, are you listening to me?" Tara asked, moving directly in front of him, cutting off the reflection of himself and most of his view of Yon'tu.

"I don't know. I...I feel like I can't breathe," he murmured, feeling his lungs growing heavier.

"Your lungs feels heavy right? You should see an indication in your mind's eye, annotating your lung PSI, etcetera. You don't see it?"

Bandares shook his head, unable to find enough breath in his lungs to respond.

"See, that's why you need the test. Lolina!" Tara called out, with her head tipped towards him, giving him a warm, knowing look.

A few seconds later, the same woman who'd first come to his barrack's chamber appeared in his field of vision, standing next to Tara. The look she had on her face made him feel like a bug or similar creature, making him question why someone with that kind of demeanor would be in charge of placing implants.

"She'll fix it. She's one of the best and definitely more trustworthy than the ship's network performing the procedures," Tara said, patting Lolina on the shoulder.

Bandares's implants reveled that Lolina was a Tier three, Ground Assault Elite as well as second in command of the brigade, with the nick name 'Ice doctor'.

"Figures," Bandares mumbled, after reading it.

"What's that?" Tara asked, pursing her lips, giving Banderas the impression she enjoyed mocking him.

"Figures her name is 'Ice Doctor'. Why are you here though? Are you here just to watch me suffer?"

"Nope, I'm here to help alleviate your pain. And his," Tara said, shooting a thumb over her shoulder in Yon'tu's direction.

Bandares slightly tilted his head in confusion then blinked, and Tara seemed to understand that he wanted her to elaborate.

"The two of you are my special cases when it comes to implants. Have you forgotten about your malfunctioning implants already?"

Bandares hadn't forgotten, but he'd yet to figure out the scope in which her painful adjustment increased his interface with them. He was going to say as much and ask more about Yon'tu as well as how the pollutants he recalled her mentioning affected his implants when something odd happened. It began with a strange sensation travelling up his spine, into his head. Then, both Tara and the 'Ice Doctor's' face grew concerned. When Lolina opened her mouth, he heard:

"Sim slesses la? Losest bama tu vless na sa su."

Then, he heard Tara respond, "Chee es nabu! Lentese ma unte fanela!"

When he didn't respond, both women bit their fingers, drawing blood, then pressed them against his chest. The odd sensation that had travelled up his spine, into his head, moved downwards towards their thumbs until he could see two large lumps underneath his skin, directly beneath their thumbs.

"Nod your head if you understand me," Lolina said in a tone that made her nickname seem totally fraudulent.

Bandares nodded his head, and saw both women breathe a sigh of relief.

"Okay, good. Your implants were under attack again. This time the target was your birth implants," Tara said, sounding exhausted.

"I felt like I was…sleeping but slipping away is the only way I can describe it. And just now, shouldn't I've been able to understand what you two were saying?"

"If we were speaking Imperial standard, yes. But we speak our own tongue for comfort and your implants auto translate. Let me guess, your birth implants never offered you the settings to turn off auto translate?

In your mind's eye, is there an icon showing you the functions of your birth implants? It's in the form of a sacred geometric with your name and an image of your DNA entwined in the middle of it," Lolina said, staring at him with a look between confusion and surprise.

"Umm, I guess not," Banderas said as he searched his mind.

"I see files and memory locations, I don't see what you're talking about at all," he replied, giving up his search.

"Tara said you're a pain in the ass. You're turning out to be more work than Yon'tu. You're lucky though, if your auto translate ever turned off, you'd have had to learn a lot of languages real fast to keep up," Lolina said, biting the bottom of her lip as if she were deciding something important.

"Bandares, we have to leave what we just collected inside of you. If we remove it or try to move it any further, none of us will survive to say what went wrong," Tara said.

"Uhh okay," he replied nervously, not knowing what to say.

All he could infer from his situation so far was from the profuse amount of sweat coming down their faces. Noticing that the longer they held their thumbs over the lumps, the more exhausted they became.

"You okay? I can take over Tara. You did enough body alchemy today. Don't you think?" Lolina whispered to Tara.

"I'm okay, so did you, taking care of Yon'tu alone for so many hours before I got here. Let's do it together. Come on, big push," Tara replied as a golden light materialized from her thumb which then dug into the left side of his chest, traveling across his heart and lungs, exiting out the right side of his chest, into Lolina's thumb.

Where the two lumps had been, he could now see dark grey and black metallic imprints. On the right hand side, a depiction of the Adrasteia binary system. On the left, the Gas giant Tepeu with fourteen orbit rings and small dots indicating its moon-worlds, with the seventh moon-world of Ah Tabai standing out from the rest.

"This is war-markings," he said, surprised and honored.

"Don't get cocky, we plan to make you earn your marks, but we figured we might as well place yours now since we had to bind the two metals trapped in your body. We depicted the Gas giant Tepeu because that's where we're heading first. Our Empress wants to bring all the moon-worlds back under Adrasteia's rule, starting with the moon-world of Ah Tabai, which is why we made it stand out amongst the rest," Tara said, flashing him prideful grin.

"Two kinds of metal? I see, that's why you asked me if I saw something metallic moving in the sludge river when we'd first meet. So the metals were going inside of my body the whole time? To me, that sounds almost like its cognitive...anyways, thank you both. My head feels so much better, clearer, and I can see a lot more interface option in my main menu. I can even see the sacred geometric with my name and DNA entwined," Banderas said, straining his eyes and neck to get a better look at his chest.

"He used to be so formal with women. Now, he talks to us like we're his equals. You see what happens when you give people special treatment?" Lolina whispered, giving him a playful wink.

"Ha, that's funny! I had called him out on that the day before! Hey Bandares! No dozing off, I see your eyes closing," Tara said, loud enough to make his ears ring again.

"I'm just thinking."

"About my question of how one would still end up in the void after an attack, even if the compartment auto depressurizes directly after being ruptured?"

"No...well...yes. They'd get tossed out from momentum. Our voidships are spinning at similar speeds to our respective planets. But our voidships are not connected in one piece even though it appears that way from outside. When a location is hit, the portion of the voidships slows or stops its spin all together, then out you go," Bandares said flatly, as he thought.

I've seen Lolina and many other women that arrived with her completely nude, and none of them had a single war marking, unlike like my previous unit commanders who had so many tattoos and metallic renderings I could barely tell the color of their skin...why is that? And I refuse to believe what's inside my body is just metal, I need to find out more.

"Ha! Not bad, at least you tried to visualise it. You have a long way to go, but for saying momentum, I'm sending you some credit in the void understanding category. This credit will go towards your next Tier promotion. See it?"

Bandares saw a three dimensional orb form in his mind. At the top of the orb, it read Tier two, and at the very bottom, the orb began to fill with a warm indigo color.

"I see it," Banderas replied, bewildered how far he had to go before making it to Tier two.

"Hey, your eyes look like they're closing again. Seriously, if you sleep you'll die. Already out of the near hundred thousand of you I picked up, some fifteen thousand have died during this procedure. If you die, the seal we put on those metals in your chest will fade. Lolina and I, along with Yon'tu will die with you before the computer or anyone else even has time to space the chamber."

"Are you making this up? If I'm this much of a threat, why use me for combat services? I'd figure they'd throw me in the mines, use me up, then toss me to the bottom of the two thousand foot deep sludge ocean. I'm sure whatever you're saying couldn't happen if I was sunk to the bottom of it. And what kind of metals behave like this anyway?"

"The Empire doesn't work like that. Hold on, I'm uploading what's known about the two metals to you now. Study this along with the alchemy you denounced so vehemently earlier."

"I truly believe body alchemy works. The show of force convinced me of that, but me harboring these supposedly dangerous metals in my body, how or why is this acceptable for the Empire? And maybe off topic, but I haven't seen any women with war markings even though, well, I'm not sure if the women belonged to your-"

"You'll find out all about our war markings later. As for your situation, it's not just you experiencing this. Whatever the metals are, they're showing up in more and more people, including myself, Lolina, and Yon'tu over there. Yon'tu's just happened to have a much more extreme case than ours.

In his case, the metals had taken over more crucial functions of his body, especially his liver," Tara replied, cutting him off before he could finish asking if the women he saw in the barrack's chambers or in the passageway belonged to her brigade or if they possibly belonged to some of the others.

"Okay, I'll take a look," he muttered, opening the file Tara sent, immediately cringing at the sheer amount of scientific information filled with words and phrases he'd never heard of.

"Yhea, I'll read it over soon," he forced himself to say, closing and moving the file to a storage location he'd never use.

"No, he's not," he heard Lolina mumble.

"He will. When he gets scared."

"Hey!" Lolina shouted, chuckling and shaking her head at Tara's cruel taunt towards him.

"Please, tell me more about what's inside me. Why is it affecting my implants? And what happened just now? I don't recall ever having that feeling before," he said, hoping what they told him would be enough for him to have an excuse to never open the file Tara gave him.

"Once the metals enter our body, it attacks anything it considers foreign, such as our implants. So anyone who has these metals in their body need to have them alchemically sealed. There are two ways to do that. The way we did it, which requires two or more casters and raw life-blood, or one caster using the material of her cycle because it's already undergone the full alchemic process, both spiritually and physically."

"So women are exhausted and feel ill during their cycle because of the natural alchemic work being done within the body?" He asked rhetorically, which gained him mocking looks from both women.

"Okay, I get it. And I truly see that you had my best interest in mind when you were planning to trigger your cycle in the temple. But why'd the metals attack me so strongly just now, and not before?" Bandares asked, trying to remember the first time he encountered the metals as a child.

"I see, Lolina was right. You're really not going to read it. Okay, listen up. When the metals enters a person's body, it slowly begins to replicate. When there's enough of it, it begins to fuse with and mutate your body. That's why we can't remove it. Your body is relying on it right now, and until we figure out how it's changed you, there's no way we can start to even slowly remove it.

The reason why it's attacking you so forcefully now is because you're right, the metals seem to be cognitive. It knows we would try to study what it's done to you over different periods of time. In order to prevent that, it behaved erratically, taking over different parts of your body as quickly as it could, destroying the timeline or steps it's taken in your body thus far."

"Yhea but, both of you-"

"Shuush, let me finish. There's another more concerning reason why we can't take it out. If we began to take it out and no adverse effects happened with your organ functions, the metals would still react once they realised they were being purged. Within seconds, they'd take over all of your motor functions and you'd become a partially living zombie controlled by them.

If this happened, you'd have immense, uncontrollable power and you'd be able to kill us and a lot more before the ship or someone could isolate you and suck you out into the void. Even in the void, you'd be partially alive because the metals would protect your body. So the powers that be would have to wait until you were frozen solid. Once you were frozen solid, Overseers and scientist would start cutting you into strips while you're still floating in the void, analyzing you piece by piece."

Hearing Tara describe everything was mortifying, but it only made Bandares even more curious as to why he'd be used as a ground assault unit who could possibly be killed at any time, only to be reborn as a zombie controlled by cognitive metals.

"So I can't fully die even when they're cutting me to strips? And you mean to tell me if I take mortal wound or tamper with the metals in any way they don't like, I'll have a fate worse than death? Where I'm alive, feeling pain and misery but unable to escape it because somehow the metals would keep me alive forever? And why do you keep saying me, if everyone in this chamber has the same metals inside them?"

"Oh, no! You'd die eventually. There appears to be a threshold of living human cells that must be maintained in order for the metals to continue to operate, which is why they fight to keep the body alive so fervently. Look, you may not understand this reasoning, but from what I've seen so far, they're not dissecting us now because we're living experiments. The Empire wants to watch us go into battle and see what happens if we die fighting or what happens to the enemy if we are captured, tortured and executed, etcetera. As a matter of fact, remember when you were eavesdropping on me speaking to the priestess about fodder for war?"

"I apologise. I…"

"Whatever. The reason I was talking about fodder and useless people is because I was mad… mad because I know I'm fodder. She's fodder. You're fodder. We're all just Imperial fodder. I've seen what they do to people with the metals in their body, void dissections and all. And I've seen how they send people with the metals in their body on suicide missions to hostile worlds, all just to catalog how fast and how many people became berserker zombies. Then they'd calculate how many of the enemy they were able to take down before they were finally taken out, if they were even taken down at all. Some are still lose upon those worlds reaping mass destruction as we speak."

"She dodged my question. Somehow I'm different than them. Her story was almost seamless till she made a slight mistake in disassociation about our fates when it comes to dying. She said I'd kill them if I became a zombie. Not I'd kill them, essentially turning them into zombies as well. She probably didn't know she made the distinction till I asked her.

I can see she's not a good liar, but she's not a mean person, so I'm not going to press her. If anything, she was trying to be nice, saying 'we' all share the same situation so I don't feel alone. But sweet or not, it's obvious to me that I'm the only person in this chamber harboring the monsters," he thought, folding his lips under his teeth, trying to figure out what made him different, if she was really telling the truth about all of them having the same metals in their body.

"Shussh. The ship can hear us. Or should I say she can," Lolina said, giving Tara a disdainful look.

"Meehe, she's already had enough of me I bet. Right sweetie?" Tara asked in an overly friendly tone of voice.

"Right," a mournful female voice replied through the chamber PA, startling Bandares as well as Lolina, seeing from the way she'd just jumped.

"Medical Emergency, Medical Emergency. Multi deck Medical Emergency. All hands with high Tier medical experience and all able bodied priestesses come to the following decks, uploading to implants now," a calm male voice said over the ships PA.

Bandares watched the women's faces go from serious to dark and mischievous.

"Lolina, I'll be back in a few. I know you can handle them," Tara said, stepping back shaking her head, then smiling at the two of them, giving Bandares the feeling he was out the loop.

"Hey Bandares," he heard Tara say as she walked out of his line of sight.

"Humm?" He mumbled, trying figure out how the two women were connected to the medical emergency.

"We both trust you have common sense. That you know how to regard us when we are around other people, yes?"

"Yes, General!" He replied sharply.

"Good, good, but that's not what I was getting at actually. Lolina and I have a reputation to uphold as evil bitches. So don't go telling people I get all sappy about everyone being fodder or that she got all motherly like when those metals were attacking your birth implants.

People need to know that she's always disconnected and level headed when she's treating the injured. And it's my job to lead us all into the meat grinder. I don't want people knowing I actually give a damn about their lives."

"Yes General!" He replied again.

"Good, good. And you, don't go telling people this either, okay sweetie? I know you're still there."

"Mmhum," he heard the mournful female voice mumble over the chamber PA, followed by a long regretful sigh.

Afterwards, he heard the hiss of the blast door open and shut, leaving Lolina standing in front of him with a dubious look on her face.

"What?" He asked, wondering if she was just saying she could handle Yon'tu and himself alone, but didn't believe her own words.

"Oh, nothing, it just wasn't the reaction I was expecting from her."

"From Tara? Or the woman who spoke over the PA?"

"Both. Speaking of which, now that your implants appear to be working correctly, do a voice match, or search who was using the chamber PA channel. See what it says."

Banderas was able to find out who the woman was after a few seconds of navigating within his new-found functions. Staring at the picture and reading the woman's bio, all he could say was, "Oh."

"Exactly. Okay let's focus on our own situation. Can you feel this?"

"Unnt unn."

"How about now?"

"Ah huhh."

"Good. How about this?"

"Yup. Hey what happened after I went into stasis? All I remember is a bunch of evil looking people and then this. At first I thought I was like this because of them," Bandares said, feeling energy returning to his body.

"Can you feel this? And don't worry about it, Tara took care of everything already. That's all you need to know. Hey, hold on, I don't think you felt that one. Ball your fist. Good."

As Bandares balled his fist, he had a flashback of punching someone as they pushed him into the stasis pod and he remembered the man had his armor unsheathed around his groin area, with an erect kudock sticking out.

A sinking, sickening feeling hit his stomach, or what he could feel of his stomach, then he thought.

"I see why Tara decided to have everyone receive their upgrades now. We're all drugged up, we can't feel a lot of pain or if we did feel some pain from what happened to us, we'd all think it was related to the intestinal implants. Her plan was really smart and also very kind. It almost made me forget everything…almost."

"Hey? Are you okay? I feel like you're trying to sneak a nap on me. These tests can't function if you're incoherent. To elaborate, your instalments will misfire in your dreams without proper calibration, reacting to things such as emotional reflexes. If you didn't understand why you needed to stay awake earlier, I hope that your guts ripping open in your dreams will frighten you enough to stay awake."

"Oh, I'm awake," he said, feeling the sinking emotion as it morphed into pure anger.

"Can you tell me what you know about," Bandares paused, knowing if he asked the question, Lolina would know he knew what had happened to him, but he felt the words slipping out of his mouth before he could stop them, "about body hosting?"

"Oh…umm. Why?"

Hearing Lolina's tone, he could tell she wanted to deflect, which actually mad him solidify his decision.

"Let's skip this please. You know exactly why. I want to be part of the reason there's another multi-deck medical emergency if people ever find a way to do that to me again," Bandares said wholeheartedly as he forced himself to recall the faces of the men and women who'd stood in front of his stasis pod.

"So you remember? Hey look…" Lolina began to say.

"I had a flashback enough to know. Please don't, don't coddle me. Please tell me what I need to know so that I may kill anyone that finds an opportunity to do this to me again."

"Okay Bandares, but the path you're choosing is a life of misery. Saying you're willing to inflict yourself with vectors to kill or harm others, is way different than saying you want to merely kill whoever has done you harm. What you're doing is giving up a piece of yourself on the off chance people will be able to do that to you again, but I think you know that don't you?" Lolina asked softly.

"Yes," Bandares murmured, feeling tears running down his cheeks as the image of the peoples' evil faces solidified in his mind.

"I bet they had a lot of pieces of me…and what do you mean, I've chosen a path of misery? I didn't choose to be taken. I…I'm still a vir…virgin. Or maybe now, now I should say I was a virgin," he stammered, wondering if his life would've been better if he'd grown up with the mentality of the people he'd been surrounded by for ten cycles.

"So tell me, am I really giving up that much of myself by wanting to host so that I may take immediate revenge on people willing to take pieces of me as they please?"

"I just fear you don't understand that asking to host is essentially a form of attracting this to happen to you again. Feeding negative emotions only bring more negative events to validate those feelings. There are so many other good and happy things you could focus on. Especially since many people such as Tara and myself have already done plenty to gain retribution for what was done to every single one of us as we were put into stasis."

"What are you talking about? How can you say that to me? Me attracting negative things to me! Never! Never! Never! I'm always trying to be happy! Always trying to be nice! Now look at what's happened to me! Tell me how I've attracted this to happen to me? They've already taken a piece of me!

So tell me! Is asking for the means to harm people who'll definitely do this to me again if they have the opportunity really giving away a piece of myself or asking for something negative like this to happen to me again? Asking to host is my way of trying to reclaim myself by gaining retribution! Is that really wrong? Or do you still think I'm asking for too much?" Bandares wailed, sobbing uncontrollably as he remember the agonizing feeling of the man inserting himself just before the stasis drugs took effect.

"No…no I suppose not," Lolina whispered, cupping his face, wiping tears away from his cheeks with her thumb.

Chapter VII

Blown out, recreated

TARA FELT TRAPPED IN A web of complex emotions as she strode through the voidship passageways. Leaving Bandares behind in the medical chamber made her feel an odd sense of emptiness, which made her happy and uncomfortable all at the same time. She couldn't even convince herself not to open a live image feed in her mind just to check on his progress. When the feed opened, she wasn't prepared to see him crying, or for him to ask Lolina about parasite hosting.

"Already he's becoming darker, and I can't blame him one bit," she thought, looking around passageways at the men and women succumbing to vectors she'd cast into them.

Stepping over a woman in battle armor that had one of the many Adrasteia Empire trident brigaded crest, she could see blue yeast fungus running out her nose as well as permeating through the whites of her eyes and into portions of her face where her sinus pathways connected to her nose and eyes.

"Oooh, that's not pretty," she said, making sure she let the woman see her smiling face glaring down at her before moving off.

"They should have known better than to mess with my brigade," she thought, shaking her head in amusement, shoulder-checking the medical team rushing to the woman's aid.

"Micro-meteorite, and particulate matter is Tier Ten-highest density. Brigade void drills are prohibited at this time," a woman said over the ships PA in a neutral tone.

Tara couldn't help but smile at the announcement, knowing that the R'yu troops in her brigade were probably throwing a tantrum at the news. Arriving at the sub chamber of the ships' bridge, Tara paused, wondering what she was going to say or do next.

"General, may I assist you?"

"No, I am here to see Admiral Sandreaka, and I don't want to hear she can't come off the bridge. Tell her ass to unplug and get out here, is that clear?" She replied sharply to the women.

"Actually, Admiral Sandreaka is rarely on the bridge. She always walks her ships, speaking with the crew. Right now, she is in one of the medical chambers. Do you see it on your…never mind," the woman said nervously.

"Yhea, you're right, I didn't check her location; I just assumed she was here," she replied, knowing what the woman was going to say.

Turning to walk out of the sub chamber, the woman made a sound as if she wanted to say something, making Tara freeze in her tracks.

"If you have something to say, say it."

"Umm. She's not a bad person, the Admiral, she… she has a good heart. If you can just try and see it."

"What you have to worry about is not if she's a bad person, but if I am a bad person," Tara responded, turning her head just enough to flash a wicked smile before continuing on her way.

Using her implants, she traced Sandreaka's location.

"Heading to your chamber already? Tired of seeing people suffering because of the mistake you made?" She thought happily, quickening her pace.

Arriving in front of Sandreaka's chamber, the blast door slid open.

"Expecting me? I…" the words she was about to say remained stuck in her mouth as two Overseers stepped out the chamber, fixing her with looks of mild curiosity before gracefully slipping past her.

"Come in Tara," she heard Sandreaka say from somewhere deep inside the chamber.

"It sounds like she was crying," she thought, taking her first steps into the chamber.

Looking around, she could see the chamber lacked any personal affects or feel of a person's presences.

"Do you not sleep here? Or I should say do you prefer to keep all of your effects in your main voidship? Either way, usually you Admirals have all sorts of stuff in every single one of your voidship sleeping chambers…you know models and what not? Like this was first ship, second ship, and all that kind of stuff," she said, trying to figure out why the bareness of Sandreaka's chamber unsettled her.

"It's as if she is not connected with this realm - by Yoginis grace!" Tara thought in horror, seeing Sandreaka emerge from her bath chamber totally nude.

"I'm ready for your peer check. I have not altered the state of my body in anyway in the bath chamber, I was simply relieving myself. The pap kit rest on my bed and I'm prepared to answer any mental health questions you've prepared. May I request we do the Pap test first?" Sandreaka said, moving to her bed, laying down with her legs spread open.

Tara rarely felt guilty for attempting to gain retribution against people who've harmed her, but seeing Sandreaka's pale, bruised body, and smelling the infection in her kunuss even from where she stood, guilt was the only thing registering. Moving into line of sight with Sandreaka's kunuss, she took in the details of the various infections visually, then closed her eyes and identified the scents.

"How old are you Sandreaka? Eighty cycles… one hundred?"

"Seventy-six cycles."

"I thought so, only older women have some of these. Sandreaka sit up a bit," Tara said softly, sitting down on the foot of the bed, never taking her eyes off Sandreaka's kunuss.

"Sandreaka, why can I find nothing truly relevant about you in the networks?" She asked, slowly drawing ambient energy into her body.

"I'm in the system."

"Yes, yes you are. I said relevant - all it says is that you were a part of the Royal Fleet. Nothing more," Tara said, withdrawing all her body armor into her body, leaving her nude.

"Tara?"

"Sandreaka, when were you going to ask for help? Unless the Overseers. Oh I see. They're your peer group. Or were…your peer group back then."

"Tara, this is not part of a mental health assessment. I'm not having this conversation."

"There's no need for a conversation Sandreaka. It's plain for me to see, your chakra circulatory system is blown out which makes it extremely hard or even impossible for your body to heal properly. Hence the bruises you get from doing simple things, like siting, walking or laying down. And of course it's why you're having an extremely hard time clearing Venusian infections you've acquired ever since you were a young woman."

"The Empress bans all contractive and protective barriers, so many people have lifelong Venusians, what of it?"

"There's something in your armour, isn't it? It blocks people from seeing your sixty four chakra points? Now that you're nude, I can clearly see you only have three chakra points with any sort of flow in them whatsoever."

"I don't know what you're talking about. Why should I need to hide? And how would I have the means to hide?"

Tara could tell just from Sandreaka's tone that she wanted to guard the fact that Overseers were going through great lengths to protect her, including placing powerful barriers within her armor so that almost none could see she was completely unable to use body alchemy. Which made her decided to only discuss the vectors as an example of why she knew her physical health situation was not normal.

"Okay, okay. Besides your chakra points being damaged, the Her'rup virus strain visible on your lip the other day has mutated millions of time since you have contracted it. It's made itself way less painful and obvious and far more potent. As a matter of fact, it doesn't breakout in large painful external blisters anymore. The most people get now is a mild fever and slightly swollen lymph glands around the groin and throat for a few days.

This way it avoids detection for cycles after contraction, allowing itself plenty of time to sneak its way into a person brain, sperm, and egg cells. After the virus makes its way into a person reproductive cells, it attaches a protein shell that works as both a shield and an energy package tool kit, whereby it metabolizes any sugar or substance it can in order to keep the sperm swimming for three weeks and the egg from dying up to fourteen days after ovulation.

Then it regulates the hormones in a person brain, making them extremely horny so that it spreads to new partners as well as the children born after the act. If you were infected with the most recent strain, you wouldn't have been in my face bothering me over trivial matters because you'd be too busy trying to spread the virus."

"Sacrilege is not trivial, Bandares's words…"

"Yhea…yhea. I'm actually annoyed at myself for not catching such obvious cues of your physical state right at the start. Then again, subconsciously I probably did, which is why I requested to do a peer check on you in the first place," Tara said, realising another factor she hadn't considered as she thought.

This is why Overseer Katina granted me permission. She wanted me to see Sandreaka for who she was. If she'd told me to be nice, I would've pushed back because I don't like people telling me what to do, especially if someone is telling me to be nice to a person who was being an ass to me.

Checking Sandreaka's blood type, she exhaled slowly, stilling herself for what she was preparing to do.

"I've been nothing but disrespectful to you Admiral Sandreaka.

I'll try to make up for this if you'll allow it. It was my pride, and umm, I have a strange connection to that man. I truly want no harm to come to him," she blurted out, instantly feeling embarrassed and surprised at herself for opening up.

Sandreaka scoffed, and Tara saw her face take on a look of embarrassment.

"You owe me no special treatment Tara, especially after what I allowed to happen to you and your brigade. There's something wrong with our culture. And instead of putting my foot down, I was trying to justify the disgusting behavior by enabling it, if that makes any sense. So, I really don't deserve your apology in the least.

And the fact that you like Bandares, was quite clear. I should've just minded my business, but I was angry when I saw you that you liked someone. I wanted to take that from you, make you bitter and alone like me," Sandreaka whispered, turning her head away so that Tara was forced to scoot herself over to see any portion of her eyes.

"I do owe you Sandreaka, I know the story well. Sixty cycle ago, three point eight billion people, including our Empress's husband and the last two of her children sacrificed themselves fighting mysterious and powerful beings in order to rescue the Niya people, allowing them to retreat safely into our Heka system. The records say that the beings were gaining the upper hand and that the battle got desperate. It's most likely during that time when you over extend the use of your body energy performing alchemy on the energy beams and kinetic weapons in order to keep the enemy from adapting.

You were literally sacrificing pieces of your ethereal body to fight and instead of dying, you blew out your chakra circulatory system. In the end you were lucky enough to survive, but not lucky enough to heal," Tara whispered, forming the seven basic sacred geometric symbols of the major chakras in her mind before casting them out to float in the air between them.

"What are you doing? You shouldn't attempt to do that kind alchemic work on me. The cost to your body will be too high. Let me live like this. I deserve it for all the times I allowed or didn't try to stop atrocities happening aboard my voidships"

"I see…so I assumed right, the Overseers are always trying to heal and protect you since you recognise what I'm doing. Don't worry, this time it's going to work permanently. Our blood types match, and not to brag, but I'm one of the few that know how do this type of alchemy inside and out. I think we were meant to be sisters, don't you think?" Tara said, finally able lock eyes with Sandreaka's again, only to find them filling with tears.

"I set you and your brigade up to be violated. I knew…I knew those broken-minded, sick bastards were going to do that to all of you. But I hated you! I hated you because you have what I want! The life I want! I…I don't deserve this. I should've died alongside my peers that day. How my life has progressed after that battle is all based on the pity of others. Yhea you guessed right, the Overseers did do something to my armour and they are trying to heal and protect me. But of course I don't want to admit they're helping me! Even if it's blatantly obvious. You know why?"

Tara shook her head 'no', not really caring what Sandreaka was going to say next, because what she planned to do would make all the misery Sandreaka lived through a distant memory.

"Because it took me thirty cycles to heal enough to even walk correctly. And, out of some respect or honor, the Empress reinstated my command. And…it's been thirty cycles since then! And guess what? I can't climb one single Tier on my own. I mean, how could I? I can't even merge with the ship. What would be the purpose of me on the bridge? I can do nothing to help without being plugged in. I don't want to live on the pity of others! I don't want to live on the pity of others! I DON'T WANT TO LIVE ON THE PITY OF OTHERS! I should've just died! Why couldn't I have just slipped into the next life? Why?" Sandreaka sobbed.

'If you'd died that day, your ethereal body wouldn't have been in its complete form and you most likely wouldn't have been able to make it to second life. But of course you wouldn't have known the true danger of overexerting your body energy, because they don't teach this to anyone outside my solar system.

I know right now you think everything is awful, but you won't have to wait too much longer before I give you a chance to enjoy your life again. I just need to finish melding the energy I collected. But I can see from the look on your face, you want me to say something. Okay sweetie, I'll entertain your train of thought for just a bit longer," Tara thought, repressing her smile in fear Sandreaka would think she was laughing at her outburst.

"Pity of others…your old peer group grew in Tiers in the sixty cycles that passed, with some becoming Overseers whom refuse to leave you behind, even if it means they run your command for you." Tara whispered, then burst out laughing, forgetting she was trying to keep a straight face when she realised that Sandreaka was one of the luckiest people she'd ever met in her life.

"What's so, so, so funny!?" Sandreaka stammered, sobbing.

"You don't need to climb Tiers dumb ass! You have Overseers as friends, who'd do whatever you want, plus more to assert your authority! They love you to death and their loyalty to you is almost equal to the love they have to the Empress. As a matter of fact, I'm sure the Empress would lose it if she knew how much they'd do for you! In an Empire where almost everyone I meet is selfish, you're surrounded by love."

"Pity isn't love. Pity is pity. The Overseers helping me were my direct subordinates who survived because I saved them. Now they flock to me, always ready to pay back their debt. Like I saved their lives to be owed something. I saved their lives because I wanted to and because that's what a good leader is supposed to do."

Tara shook her head in disagreement at Sandreaka interpretation of the Overseers actions, but didn't want to say anything more to press her opinion.

"I tell you what then," she said, softly tugging on Sandreaka's leg letting her know she wanted her to bring them down in front of her.

"You said I owe you nothing for what you allowed to happen to me and my brigade, correct? So then, let's just say what I am about to do comes from the heart. Forget what I said about owing you respect for being in the Royal Fleet," she said, knocking the pap kit off the bed.

"You shouldn't regardless. AH!"

Tara ignored her, and commanded the seven sacred geometric energy patterns to insert themselves into Sandreaka's body.

"The trick is to also form the minor chakra points," she reminded herself, forming them into existence, then laying them into Sandreaka body.

"Stop!!! It hurts so bad! Please stop!" Sandreaka pleaded.

Moments after she'd begun the procedure, Tara heard people rushing into the chamber and within seconds she could see fifteen Overseers crowding around Sandreaka's bed and herself.

"Second trick is proper wave lengths of light mixed with the blood given by the donor," she thought to herself, vibrating her body energy until she was engulfed in a brilliant blue-white light.

Taking a deep breath, she willed her blood to flow out of her kunuss and nipples, forming three globular orbs that floated before her.

"Of my blood and my will. Of my energy and my boundless spirt," Tara whispered, adding small portions of her ethereal body into the orbs of blood before sending them to hover over Sandreaka.

"I call upon the power of thought, intention, and willpower. Let your trinity be the roots and anchor that bond myself with Sandreaka. Heal at once!" Tara screamed, infusing the three orbs of blood into Sandreaka's breast and kunuss.

Sandreaka's shrieks took on a new pitch, then died down as Tara's blood infused with Sandreaka's ethereal and physical body. With the blood now infused in Sandreaka's body, the carefully crafted energies Tara had melded rekindled all of Sandreaka's chakra points. When Tara felt comfortable with the flow of Sandreaka's chakra circulatory system, she pulsed her body energy over and over until she resembled a blinding pulsar star.

"This will clear every vector and further aid in the rejuvenation of her cells. Now all she needs is sex and Reiki," she thought, reducing the amount of energy she channeled back to her usual levels.

By the time her bodies' toural energy sphere faded back to its normal, less perceivable spectrums of visibility, the fifteen Overseers in the chamber were all staring at her. Shrugging her shoulders as if to say it was no big deal, they then turned to look at Sandreaka in a strange perfect unison, reminding her of felines tracking the same prey.

"You all know the nature of this body alchemy, correct?"

Without looking back at her, she saw them all nodded their heads once in unison.

"Good, I'll leave you all to it. I'm going to go die somewhere now," she said sarcastically, feeling the first side effects hit her as she moved closer to Sandreaka, who had her arm out, reaching for her.

"Hey there. How does it feel to have a piece of me inside you? You said you were jealous of me. Now you can't be, right sister?" She asked meekly, taking hold of Sandreaka's out stretched arm along with her hand.

"Thank you…I really appreciate you. And not to dampen the mood, but why? You know we're on our way to death right? You know who we are up against right? The beings who attacked the Royal fleet, their origins have been traced back to the moon-world of Ah Tabai. When you make land fall, you will need all your strength."

Tara felt a slight pang of fear hearing Sandreaka's words, her prior briefs had only focused on human targets on Ah Tabai. Hearing that wasn't the case and that her brigade was to be put up against mysterious beings the Empire had yet to disclose the identity of, wasn't something her mind had been ready for. When she realised the logic behind why only five Elite brigades where chosen to make land fall on Ah Tabai before all other Imperial forces, her dark sense of humor kicked in.

"It's okay Sandreaka, everything is working out for all of us. There's no we, and you know it. All the briefs say you're just dropping us off in a prime location you deem fit, then you're getting out of there. If there's any trouble in the void, you're now healthy enough to fight and take proper vengeance against these beings.

So if you do somehow end up dying, at least your life will end on the note of closure. The best part is that after you drop us off, you'll be ridding the Empire of some of its most broken minded, yet useful war tools, who think of violating others as a pass time. Surely the Empress knows what she's doing when she choose the five most vicious Ground Assault Elite commands in the Empire to begin this war yes?"

Sandreaka smiled weakly, and Tara could see the color of her face was already looking healthier.

"You're twisted Tara, or should I say Blue Star. But what do you get out of this. You said it works out for all of us. I only heard something for me and for the Empress."

"Me, well I made a powerful new friend, I can dare call sister. And-" Tara kissed Sandreaka's hand, then moved her lips to Sandreaka's mouth.

Just before kissing her, she tilted her head and whispered in Sandreaka's ear, "and since you're not going to kill or hurt my Bandares for his words anymore, I'm going to make the best of the time I have with him before we both die on that stupid planet."

When Tara lifted her head from the kiss, she saw Sandreaka had already fallen sound to sleep.

"Empty chamber because she was dead on the inside," she thought as she called out her body armour.

"General Blue Star. Would you like one of us to walk with you? You've used much of your energy and-"

"And the other brigades are looking for an opening for some good old retribution for that nasty spell I cast into them, even though they all know they had it coming. And whereas before you couldn't give a damn what happened to me or my people, now that I saved your precious Sandreaka, you feel you owe me? Humph, I'm starting to see...never mind. I'm fine walking alone. Thank you," she said firmly, making sure she pushed and shoved as many Overseers as she could on her way towards the chamber blast door.

Stepping through the door as it opened, she called over her shoulder "oh, and I cleared all of your disgusting Venusians as well, so make her healing session special."

When the blast door closed, she smiled and mumbled "and I rejuvenated her eggs and triggered her ovulation. I'll be damned if she goes back to war."

"Transport voidship merge with main void sphere 'Voice of Kali' T-minus two minutes. Tier four Brigade Generals are requested to come to the chamber of 'Kali's Embrace' on main void sphere for briefing," a soft female voice said over the ship's PA.

"Damn it! I'm tired. I need a bath, and the last people in the universe I want to see right now are the other Generals," she grumbled, knowing the real reason she was annoyed was because it was ruining her plan of returning to see Bandares.

"Reopen live feed to medical chamber of the 'Devoted follower'," she mumbled under her breath as she changed passageways, directing herself towards a lift that would integrate with the main voidship, bringing her closest to the chamber of 'Kali's Embrace'.

"What do you think the meetings about?" Lolina asked in her mind as she walked.

"I see he is all patched up. Yukk, what kind of sick game is that? It's making my skin crawl!" She proclaimed, seeing Bandares match parasites with their proper eggs on a holo-imager.

"Fastest way for him to learn about hosting."

"Yunnhuh. Or be dissuaded from it, which I know is what you're hoping for. Okay, talk soon," she said, arriving at the lift.

"Why are you kicking me out of your head so fast? You want to spy on him in silence?" Lolina retorted.

"Actually…yes," she replied truthfully, bursting out laughing once she'd heard what she wanted to do stated to her so matter of factly.

Stepping into the lift, it quickly dropped down hundreds of levels then stopped. Stepping off, she made her way through three blast doors before arriving in the chamber 'Kali's Embrace' which was designed in the likeness of a tunneling drill.

"Welcome, welcome. Now that all five of you are here, we can begin."

"You've got to be kidding me," she thought, not believing her eyes as she took in the woman's features.

"As all of you have probably guessed from my fair skin, high cheek bones, narrow eyes, and long black hair, I'm of Niya origin. Well it used to be all black, I'm going a little grey now," the woman said nervously.

"Anyways, I am not into Imperial formalists. My name is Lanying, and that's it. No Lord General, no Ground Assault Elite, I'm just Lanying. So take a seat and open your minds as much as you can, and I'll tell you as much as I can about the beings you are to face when you arrive at the moon-world of Ah Tabai."

Tara looked at the other Generals' faces, and saw they were just as dumbfounded as she was.

"Excuse me? Beings? Ah Tabai is a world filled with giant people sure, but I don't classify that as beings. What do you mean beings? None of us were told of this!" A Generals named Oma'na retorted.

"Ladies, sit or when I touch your minds you'll find yourself on the floor a different way."

"You're a Mind-Bender," Tara said, sitting down quickly.

"Whatever you say child," the woman whispered as a violet glowing orb formed in front of her forehead, jumping into each of the General's foreheads before entering hers.

"There are seven sentient beings all of you need to be aware of. The first three live, for the most part symbiotically. From what we know, which is still very little, life for these three beings start with one type of spore which somehow then gives birth to two more individual organisms. The first being that emerge from the spore are tree-like beings that we Niya have named the 'Mu-waiqiao'. Now as I said before, the next two beings seem to be born out of the tree-like beings.

But here's the thing, they only appear during certain stages of the tree-like beings life. When the Mu-waiqiao are healthy, beings that resemble beetles come forth. There are a wide variety of these beings as well, with many shapes, sizes, colors, etcetera. Overall, we call them the 'Jiachong-waiqiao'. Once the Jiachong-waiqiao leave the tree, they usually set up their own technologically advanced cities and have even been seen as the dominant species on a couple of planets we Niya have kept an eye on. Any questions so far?"

Tara already had thousands, mostly having to do with the fact that she believed Lanying was contradicting herself by saying they knew very little, yet uploading so much information into her mind about the two beings she'd just mentioned.

"All of you are already overwhelmed I see. Okay ladies, keep your minds flexible, this brief is only going to intensify. I will now discuss these yellow, larva-like beings that come forth when portions or when the entire Mu-waiqiao is dying. Be extremely careful with them. The way they look visually is very deceptive from the way they move. They may look bulbous, soft and slow, however, their bodies are made liquid metal. Actually, truth be told, all three of these beings are mostly composed liquid metal cells."

"Excuse me, liquid metal cells?" A General name Ro'sen'ka blurted out.

"Yes, so far we've counted a little over two thousand different types of metallic cells, many of which the most brilliant alchemic scientist have a hard time comprehending. I mean, it's common sense to know that there needs to be a variety of cells to build a living being. For example, we humans are composed of over two hundred different types of cells. But I myself find it hard to comprehend thousands of functioning living metallic cells," Lanying said softly, nodding her head in Tara's direction.

Which oddly made Tara feel reassured that in the grand scheme of things, the awful vibe she was picking up from Lanying, wasn't all that bad in comparison to something non-human and dangerous.

"In the case of these yellow larva-like beings we call 'Jiangshi-waiqiao', alchemic material scientist have only been able to make proper structural models representing three types of metal cells found in their body. Any questions?"

Tara slowly shook her head in a 'no', even though she was thinking, *"hurry up, I want to know more!"*

"But as Generals I'm sure that's not all that interesting, so let's focus on their behavior. From what we've observed, they appear to live for the sole purpose of attacking anything and everything near the Mu-waiqiao's injured area. If you want a reference, picture how our white blood cells behave when we're cut. This reference ties into an important fact to know for immediate retreat purposes. Sometimes, if an entire Mu-waiqiao is dying, the Jiangshi-waiqiao have been known to swarm so thick into the void that they've created their own gravitational pull. I feel I don't need to say any more in regards to why you should immediately flee."

"We're never supposed to re-," Tara heard a Generals named Xes'kiko start to say, but Lanying didn't miss a beat cutting her off when she said.

"You may die and kill your brigade as you wish Xes'kiko, but I have a feeling you'll change your mind after I finish discussing them. All of you listen very carefully. When these beings attack humans, the first thing they do is liquefy and enter our bodies, turning us into zombies. The worst part is that once they take you, they gain full access into your mind, implants, coms, just literally everything. The information they gain, they also share freely amongst the other two beings.

So Xes'kiko, do you still believe you or your peers should stick around in front of a swarm that can throw planets out of orbit, all to waste life on honors sake? Besides it's not just wasting you and your brigade's life. All five of you know all kinds of vital Imperial information such as troop movement, logistic issues, and everything else. Also, many of you are masters of particular forms of alchemy. Should honor be the reason that all of this is lost and compromised?"

Seeing the images and hearing the capabilities of the beings, Tara felt her heart pounding so hard it made her lungs rattle as she thought.

"I get how Bandares felt when I gave him the file on the metals inside our bodies. Hey wait a minute! Metallic cells! Let me check that file and my own personal study files to see if there's any connection!"

"Next we have beings that resemble jellyfish, which we call the 'Haizhe-waiqiao'. Their behavior is very hard for us to predict, and they seem to appear only after a certain time period in which the other three beings become locked in combat with either themselves or other beings, such as humans. Their primary attack is to simple engulf and literally eat us, armor, ships, everything. Such as this case here, where you can actually see this Void Assault troop in her single person pod being digested."

Tara flinched in horror seeing the voidship along with the woman's body dissolving in the translucent form of the being.

"None of the beings she's shown so far have metallic cell properties coming anywhere near close to a match to the metals being found in people's bodies, unless something is missing from the files she's sending. Or maybe I've failed to understand what I was seeing during my own analysis."

"Moving on to the next three beings. I should say we loosely classify as beings, since we really can't tell what they are. These three are also made up of metallic cells. But here's the biggest problem, two of them only ever appear like this."

Tara saw an oily black orb, then a dark silver orb appear in her mind, causing the hairs on the back of her neck to stand up.

"As you can see, two orbs of liquid metal is not much to go by. So the black orb we have named 'Heiyeti-shenmi' and the silver 'Yinyeti-shenmi'. Keep these two orbs in mind for the last being I'll show all of you later on," Lanying said, looking directly at her as a file uploaded into her mind, saving her the effort of combing through the other files any further.

"I'm usually pretty good at assuming, but this one was way over my head. I'd

thought the Empire was dumping the metallic cells into the oceans and rivers to experiment on a large populace, possibly to see if people would mutate into anything useful. But now I see the metals are loosely classified as sentient beings! Knowing their origin is sentient is way worse than if they were just cognitive creations cooked up in some lab. Sentient beings have time, experience, imaginations, willpower, and lots of motive adding to their cognitive ability. I need to learn how to do more than just bind them!" She thought frantically, feeling her eyes water as she thought about the implications of having metal based sentient beings trapped within her body.

"Tara, let's speak after the briefing," Lanying said, snapping her out of her mulling thoughts, in which she tried to retrace her steps as a child, wondering if she could've done anything different to avoid being exposed to the metals, even though she already knew she wouldn't have been able to since it undoubtedly would've been in her food and water supply.

As a reply, she simply nodded her head, wanting Lanying to continue, hoping she'd discuss if there were ever any sightings of the metallic orbs landing into the oceans and rivers of Imperial controlled planets.

"Okay, so I'm going to back track a bit because talking about the last being is difficult without clearer context of the others. So now that all of you have the basic idea of what six of the beings are, let's go into more depth about the tree-like beings since they make up sixty percent of the surface area of Ah Tabai and ninety percent of its subsurface. Since we all know Ah Tabai is ninety five percent water, you can see why I think discussing them is top priority."

Lanying formed images of Ah Tabai in her mind in such great detail, she almost felt as if she were already there.

"The Mu-waiqiao are just as diverse in culture, appearance, and belief systems as humans. Unfortunately for humans, only a few like us. After my people arrived in Heka system sixty cycles ago, my people along with your people's, Overseers, and Infiltrator units, monitored the moon-world of Ah Tabai to see if they were going to follow suit and attack, without provocation as they had to my people and countless other human, and other sentient being civilizations."

"Without provocation?" Tara muttered, shaking her head at what she considered an obvious lie.

"I should say there were maybe a few minor provocations on the Niya part."

"Minor huh…they almost wiped out every living soul in your previous Empire, now all of you are part of Adrasteia, whether you people like it or not," she said firmly, annoyed that Lanying always made strong distinctions between Niya and Adrasteia people.

"Anyways, all of us almost came to the conclusion that they were going to leave Adrasteia binary alone, and we were happy not to make a move against them. Especially since we knew what a direct fight with them could costs in lives and resources in just a mere matter of minutes. Then came the bad news.

Infiltrator units sent to the surface of Ah Tabai had come to find out that many of the Mu-waiqiao were implementing a new strategy to deal with humanity, which was to merge their bodies with our own. Essentially creating symbiotic colonies of four different beings, with the human body as the main structural frame for the other three beings. If that doesn't make sense, here are a few images of people who have undergone a full merge."

Tara squinted, thinking about what she'd just heard as she studied the images of people with smooth metallic skin resembling vegetation, in different hues of green, blue, and brown. Inside some of the people's arms and backs, she could see honeycomb structures housing the 'beetle like' Jiachong-waiqiao. Then she took note of the various yellow patches on the heels of peoples' feet where she figured the 'larva-like' Jiangshi-waiqiao resided.

"Soooo, they can shrink at whim?" A General beside her named Besa said, beating her to it.

"Yes indeed, since all the beings are made of metal cells, it's as simple as a thought for them to expand or contract volume of material making up their bodies. As long as they have their brain or whatever it is they use to control life function of their body, they can maintain themselves as an individual. In certain instances we have seen them shrink themselves down to the size of the smallest know single celled bacterium."

"Umm…Lanying. Is symbioses really an attack? Many organisms live like this. Actually viruses, fungi, and bacterium are living in us right now doing something quite similar or maybe even more invasive. Is this premise of why this merge constitutes as an attack? All because of its similarity with the way organisms live within us now?

If yes, then my question is, what has made this classified as an attack against all humans in Adrasteia binary? Because if I follow this logic, then the bacteria and fungi that feed and breed on the yogurt and honey I jam into my troops kunusses when they have yeast infections constitutes as a bacteria, fungi merge attack with the female body.

Maybe the people of Ah Tabai want to live like this for quality of life reasons. Just because the beings they live with are visible doesn't make it any less different than how we choose to live with the invisible organisms inside our body right now," Tara said, wondering why anyone in their right mind would want visible insect like beings living inside their body, but unable to put it past a person, knowing from personal experience that one person bliss was another's nightmare.

Tara heard chuckling and before she could snip at the other Generals, Besa said.

"For the rest of my life I'll picture Ah Tabai as the world which represents yeast infection that should be cured with a Tier one bombardment of yogurt and honey."

"Besa please, be mature. Good point Tara. I should say we assume, which yes, we all know is a very dangerous word. But in this circumstance, we assume this is their way of getting to us without fighting a direct war. When your Empress rescued my people. Excuse me, I meant to say our Empress. When our Empress rescued us, she found and exploited what appeared to be a major weakness in the final phase of the battle."

Tara gave Lanying the evilest look she could muster.

"Excuse me for my slip of tongue earlier, old habits die hard. She is without a doubt our Empress and we are without a doubt, one people. So please bear with me when I say my people, I mean it in the context of this topic. I promise all of you, since our rescue and to this very day, we all love and embrace Adrasteia with all our hearts."

Tara picked up the malice and disgust in Lanying's tone for even having to associate herself with Adrasteia, and wondered why the Empress bothered to rescue the Niya. Even more so, she couldn't fathom why the Empress would still put up with them since she was certain the Empress could see through any fake loyalty the Niya people presented to her.

"I wonder why we're just hearing about the nature of these beings now? Or the fact that they've been on Ah Tabai the entire time? From what 'my people' know about the Niya is that 'your people' got their asses handed to them by powerful beings, but not what kind of powerful beings. Any historical documents I've ever dredged up on the battle we fought to save your people's sorry asses, the beings were labelled either 'the enemy' or 'the mysterious powerful beings'."

"Yes well see-" Lanying began, but Tara's blood was boiling too hot to listen.

"I know I asked, but before you answer, I'm going to take a

guess that the real reason these beings identities were hidden from the general public, was because the Empress wanted to protect your people from being rejected and ejected out of Adrasteia controlled solar systems.

She knew if her real subjects found out that the enemy were a bunch of weird, yet beatable plant mixed with bug like beings, they would never respect or accept 'your people' for being so weak they couldn't defend themselves and had to come running to us for help," Tara said bitterly, unable to pass up an opportunity to try and harm Lanying's pride with her words.

She could hear the other Generals chuckling softly and found herself surprised they shared her exact sentiment.

"I cannot speak for our Empress. If she wanted to protect my peoples' pride and reputation. Well I…" Lanying trailed of, and Tara saw an odd emotion cross her face, that looked like she'd had an epiphany.

"Excuse me, I just realised something. So, umm, like I said I cannot speak for the Empress in regards to her decision not to classify the enemy in the past. But if your question is, why hasn't there been more preparation? Or, why all of you haven't been warned a few more months ahead this present time, I can-"

"Both," Tara said sharply, cutting Lanying off.

"Well, all of you should already inherently know that preparation is a constant. Please, always keep this in the forefront of your mind. That being said, weapons have been developed and refined for your brigades to use. I'll be distributing them to each of you personally in the next couple of hours.

Also… and this is not a promise, I'll try to have everyone transferred to the newest voidships, designed by skilled ship builders from both Niya and Adrasteia culture alike. At the moment there are still a few bugs in the systems, as well as few political problems in terms of manning. Which is a whole other long story I'll tell you individually when I bring you the weapons."

"Don't you think we need them now? We have hundreds of thousands to distribute them to, and we ourselves don't know how to use them. So don't you think we need every ounce of time to learn them, so that we may train our troops before we get to Ah Tabai," Generals Ro'sen'ka asked, and Tara could tell from her tone that she disliked Lanying even more so than herself.

"The weapons are not what any of you are picturing, so let me try to explain. I said they're refined for use, however they need to be fine-tuned first. Sounds the same but...a bit of a big difference. I'm actually in the process fine tuning them now even as we speak.

And before any of you feel like I'm holding out on you, I want you all to know something very important. The main weapons that've been forged for this fight are actually all of you. I say this because you and your brigades have been engineered for endless warfare after cycles and cycles of what your Empress...uh, our Empress deemed as necessary tough love."

Tara smiled at the fact that her twisted sense of humor turned out to be true.

"We're expendable human monsters. Great," she uttered sarcastically, recalling a painful memory from her childhood.

"I have nothing to say to that Tara...I had no say in this. Our Empress designed this system long before the Niya came under her fold. And I actually have a confession, earlier I lied when I said I don't know the reason why our Empress wished for these being not to be mentioned to the general public. I realised I was lying as I told the lie, so try to forgive me. Truth be told, we humans are the invaders.

Anyone in a position of power such as our Empress, has information assessable to her, allowing her to peer deep into humanities settlement history in this portion of the Galaxy. She could see these beings were here long before humanity even existed as a species. From the historic records, she'd see that all of us had powerful ancestors, which were Tiers ahead of where our Empire stands now. These ancestors mercilessly exterminated these beings off of thousands of worlds, afterwards settling down into the colonies that have formed the various civilizations and Empires we know to exist today."

"That sounds like good news," General Oma'na responded.

"Well see, our Empress didn't want to appear soft in the eyes of her people. Imagine the outcry if she told people the truth? That she didn't want to disturb the beings who killed three point eight billion people in ten minutes time, all to rescue the last seventeen billion of an Empire who once boasted ten trillion people.

Don't you think people would've questioned her leadership if she named an enemy living right under Adrasteia's nose, then said let's leave these beings alone, let's forget what they've done to us since it's nothing compared to what our ancestors have done to them. Let's all just live in peace with these beings like the Ah Tabai people are doing."

Lanying waited for a moment, and Tara could see her eyes mainly focusing on her, but for once Tara found herself having nothing to say.

"See none of you could say anything, because there's no chance she'd get away with it. She would've had to execute millions, if not more of her own people in a show of force just to make everyone respect her again. So it was best for her to keep the circle small in terms of who knew what happened.

That part was particularly easy for her because only about two hundred thousand of the four billion in her Royal fleet survived. And as all of you already know, we Niya pretty much stay to ourselves, even though we live on every single one of the forty six Heka moon-worlds.

This is why only our youngest come and mingle with Adrasteia's normal population. Anyone who lived through the horror these beings brought when they attacked, cannot help but bring it up, which is exactly what the Empire doesn't need. So there it is…our Empress wanted to leave the whole thing alone. She knows whenever we humans meddle with these beings, it seems to end poorly for us."

"So this is what your people call minor antagonism huh? You Niya meddled with them to the point where Adrasteia had to come save the last of your minor antagonizing, meddling asses. That's what I get out of this. And now we're fighting your old war, since your people pissed them off enough that they decided to do something treacherous in our home system. Umm, 'your people' in the contextual sense of this topic that is." Tara said, finally seeing the rise she was looking for when Lanying's face turned sour.

"Touché Tara," Lanying replied dryly after a long moment.

"So, tell us more. What did your people do to meddle with them? From what you've said and shown us so far, it seems to me they have more to gain living with humans than from killing us," Tara said, reveling in the growing discomfort playing out on Lanying face.

"In my opinion, merging is harmonization. And in my opinion as well as many others, it's a much more peaceful way to stop a war. However, our Empress doesn't think so. She believes it to be hostile, because when they merge with us, they're tainting humanity or what it means to be human. Cutting off our ability to, umm…her wording is transcend or evolve on our own."

"Dodged my question about what your people did to antagonise them real fast didn't you bitch," Tara thought, getting ready to repeat her question again, but before she had a chance to Lanying said.

"We've gone too far off topic. I wanted to give a clearer context of the six beings before I discussed the seventh and final being, which only comes at the end of a war. The best way to do that is to talk about the type of war these beings wage between each other, which in this case has nothing to do with humans.

Like I said before, we know there are different cultures, but we don't know what triggers the actual fight between the cultures, or if it's possibly even a civil war between the same two cultures. As you'll soon see, one cannot even dare go near the solar system to ask what all the fuss is about without paying the ultimate price."

When Lanying finished speaking, she smiled again, and this time Tara saw an aura of pure evil rising from the woman, as if she were thoroughly enjoying the news she was about to deliver.

"To begin with, the violence is short-lived and extremely intense as both sides will utterly annihilate each other. The beings killing each other would be fine, except...well, as you can see now."

An image appeared in Tara's mind that seemed unreal.

"This. This isn't possible," she stammered, staring at a tree branches as thick as continents reaching out into the void from what she thought looked like a moon or very small planet. The branches did not stop when they reached the void, but continued all the way to another slightly larger planet that was at least four light minutes away.

Where the branches had struck the planet, she could see lava, dust, and strange looking humanoid beings, dead and dying around them. On the outskirts of the dead and dying humanoid beings, she could see millions if not more in an array of armament from voidships to hovering tanks. She watched them fire everything they had at branches, yet nothing even left a mark and within moments she watched them all pulverised by golden specks of light bursting forth from the branches.

"Those sentient beings fighting for their home world and solar system are now extinct. They were a newly emerging Tier one civilization, doing quite well for themselves I might add. They'd just colonised their fourth terra formed moon and were in the process of terra forming a fifth, when they had the unfortunate luck of one of their terra forming engines accidently digging up a few Mu-waiqiao spores that'd been buried deep within the moon. By the way, all this destruction took place within one Adrasteian day. Behold day two."

Tara's head felt like it was going to burst trying to comprehend what she was seeing. The jelly fish-like beings that Lanying had shown them earlier had formed an organic lens-like structure, made of their own bodies, directly in front of the solar systems Blue giant sun. Without recourse, they fired intensely focused beams the same diameter and circumference of her home world.

As the beams traveled, they smashed into the branches and trunks of the Mu-waiqiao whose limbs had now stretched out across the entire solar system and had literally embedded themselves into anything and everything from solid solar system bodies to Gas giants. Once the limbs were struck by the beam, they either disintegrated or grew stronger.

If the branches grew stronger, the beetle like beings would emerge in massive swarms. If the branches had been severed, the yellow spore-like beings would erupt out in massive swarms. With only four intense energy beams having been fired so far, Tara could already see the entire solar system teeming with literally trillions of beetle and larva like beings.

"Now day three."

Tara saw a dark silver liquid orb and a shiny, oily black orb literally bursting though the Blue giant sun. Wherever flares erupted, she could see a concentration of immense energy. The two orbs released that energy towards each other, then against every other being and planet in the solar system, turning everything into fine grey dust while somehow igniting all six Gas giants to burn like suns.

"Day four."

Tara saw only sterile void, with not even a speck of dust or light. She waited and waited, wondering when Lanying was going to show what happened. Finally losing her patience, thinking something was wrong, she asked.

"Where's the dust, the sun...or umm...all seven of them? I see nothing."

"Exactly. Nothing is left. Well, almost nothing."

"That's impossible! It takes billions of cycles. There should still be something and..." Tara closed her mouth as she saw two orbs moving slowly through the sterile darkness and this time each orb contained a mix of silver metallic liquid and black metallic liquid.

While she stared at the two orbs, she felt something move inside her ankles, directly where a priestess had sealed the metals in her body.

"Oh, lives," she muttered, trembling uncontrollably in fear, realising what the metals inside her body truly were.

"And being or should I say beings number seven and eight. Unsure of what to really make of them, we call the two the Ronghuide-hei...exact Niya translation, the mix of darkness's," Lanying said, showing the orbs slowly forming into beings that had the likeness of all the living beings in the former solar system.

"From the last image I've shown you and from what they're doing on Ah Tabai, we've made the assumption that they prefer to take on images of the main sentient beings of the solar system. We've even gone so far as to guess that this war was for control of the solar system. Some with and some against a forced merge with the sentient beings of that solar system.

If we're right, we can see the ones who were against the merge did not win. Or in the end, they were forced to say yes in order to save what was left of the sentient beings, since it's obvious they weren't going to make it through their type of conflict anyway. Which is why we must fight them before any of this happens. We cannot allow these beings to make choices for us."

"We can't fight them. These beings are Tiers past us," Tara whispered.

"We can fight them! Humans have great power! Our ancestors took them down once before! Clearing away these monsters so that humanity could thrive! Not only that, but many people have sacrificed themselves to ensure we will win this war! That solar system all of you just saw was actually in the Nautilus galaxy, our dwarf galaxy orbits. Meaning it's so far away it would take millions of entanglement points to reach it."

"A hive-mind scan...all the way across this galaxy...into another, more than ten times as large," Tara murmured, feeling her palms begin to sweat realising that the act represented sheer insanity and desperation.

"Exactly so Tara! It took around three hundred million Niya simultaneously extending their consciousness to this solar system to bear witness to this event and none of them survived! But it's okay! They were all happy giving up their lives to prepare others for the war that is to come!"

"Why would they do such a thing? What could drive them to go to such lengths?" Tara wondered, watching Lanying's face change to one of maniacal rage with every new word she said.

"I hope the Empress applied enough of her tough love pressure! Your darkened vengeful souls! The new weapons I bring! And a solid will to survive! Is the only thing that can save us from utter annihilation!"

Chapter VIII

Symbiosis, Okay?

At the same time

Location: Moon-world of Ah Tabai

"ALRIGHT! I'VE GOT to admit it, you were both right to keep me from going outside the other day!" Wa'raydon shouted, just managing to move out the way of a hail storm of kinetic projectiles.

"Sorry this is happening to you son! Truly sorry! If you survive this, you'll have learned enough to know when self-preservation outweighs blind loyalty and duty," his mother replied, firing kinetic projectiles from the tips of her trident down the length of the chamber, turning the assailants rushing his position into mush.

"You should use our old Imperial standard trident son. I hate to say it, but it wasn't built with the idea of saving credits like your sword or gun. Plus it's an all-in-one weapon, since it fires projectiles and energy beams," His father lectured, just before Wa'raydon raised his gun, firing a mix of lasers and kinetic projectiles into a support beam, killing the people behind it.

"I like holding sword and gun! What's wrong with having two weapons?" He retorted angrily as he ran up and took position behind Adenetta.

In his mind's eye, he read the text: "Tracking: Six incoming. Full symbiosis, Okay?"

"No G'o, full symbiosis is not okay, show me the six," he commanded, tapping Adenetta's shoulder with the back of his sword hand, letting her know he wanted to be the one to take care of the people coming.

"You sure you're okay?"

"Yhea, I'm alright," he said, not feeling alright after seeing the six people's faces appear in his mind.

Four of the six people were the family who lived down the hall from his own, and two were from his command. With a nod to Re'meka who was on the far side of the chamber, positioned behind a support beam, he lunged past Adenetta and fired six times. As he fired, Re'meka fired rounds of explosive orb crystals to cover him. Making it over to her, he took cover and waited for the fate of the six people to flash across his mind's eye.

"No life signs detected," he read as an image appeared in his mind's eye, showing him the sprawled out bodies, each with a tiny hole through the forehead.

"It looks like something's wrong with their armor, their helmets should have auto formed as the projectiles came. Not that it would've mattered. Even with the all the tweaking they did, I still knew all of their armor settings inside and out," he thought, feeling his stomach turn as fond memories of all of them came to mind.

"Symbiosis type would be mutual. Full symbiosis, okay?" Flashed across his mind's eye again, cutting off the view of the bodies.

"No, it's not okay. You're already in my body, what more do you need?" He replied telepathically to G'o.

G'o instantly replied by showing him an image of his body with highlights of where it wanted access.

"That's my body's entire regulatory systems! And my chakra circulatory system as well! No way!" He replied telepathically, turning to give his mother and father the all clear signal to move up.

They were already moving, and he couldn't help but crack a smile knowing they were way better in ground combat situations than himself.

"Like your mother said, it's not your fault sweetie, you wouldn't have known your own troops would turn against you."

"I brought the enemy right to our faces. I should've known to wait and assess every angle within my command before bringing Adrasteia sympathisers right to us. The thing is, everything happened too quickly for my understanding. I felt no tension or uneasiness within my own troops and we spend a lot of time mind-linked. So I don't exactly know how I should've known what to look for. If that makes any sense."

"That's because the Adrasteia sympathisers did nothing hostile the entire time. They communed amongst each other casually, having mental conversations on levels none could see. The people still loyal to you didn't know they were in trouble either, correct? Doesn't that tell you something?" Re'meka replied, raising her arm, cuing Adenetta to move up.

Wa'raydon watched Adenetta move nimbly in spite of the shell-like structure holding their children attached to her back. Looking down, he examined the structure on Re'meka's back and couldn't help but shiver.

"The pouch looks like it's connected to your body," he said, un-forming his sword into his hand before touching it. "*It feels extremely hard, yet warm to the touch,*" he thought, moving his hand lower, tracing what felt like Re'meka's heartbeat.

"Is this full symbiosis with G'o?" He inquired pensively after timing the rhythm of the pulse.

"I'm protecting our children, try not to sound upset at that," Re'meka answered in a low, scalding tone.

"*Protecting our children at the expense of not being human in the end doesn't sound safe to me,*" he thought, pressing his consciousness outward to see if he could find any of his people still loyal in the general area, only to find loathing in every mind he touched.

"*Anyone who was still loyal to me is dead, just like I would've been had I gone out there. The two faced monsters were waiting to kill us in one swoop, but when I didn't go out there right after I said I would, they got impatient and decided to strike them first and find me later! Never in my life would I think I'd need to thank my mom for a trident in the foot!*"

"Damn it," he mumbled, trying to think through his situation.

"G'o: main body, no longer functioning," flashed in his mind.

"We have to get out of the building now! Son, Re'meka get over here now!" His father commanded mentally.

While his father spoke, all the views G'o had been providing throughout the building began to go blank in his head.

"Crap," he muttered, looking around the large chamber that'd served as the shopping center for the thousands who lived on the one eighty seventh level of the mega building.

Roots and branches were beginning to turn a grey sickly color, and portions of wall where the roots had merged with the structure of the building began to crumble. Taping Re'meka on top of her helmet, he rushed forward aiming in every direction. Making it to his parents and Adenetta's general location, he kneeled behind a thick piece of broken pillar and felt Re'meka as she kneelt behind him, pressing her shell like pouch against his back.

"What's the plan, since airborne is not an option? Especially now that the fence of voidships I called to protect us is now the fence trapping us in here," Wa'raydon said darkly.

Re'meka began firing, and even though the gun fired silently, the damage it was causing further down the chamber was anything but.

"We still need to get to the lifts and go underground," his mother said, not sounding too convinced of the plan herself.

"Mom, what's with the tone?" He asked, moving G'o's message to the side of his mind's eye, which was now flashing over and over in amber and red.

"G'o isn't dead yet. It's collecting the last of its energy to protect us. It was trying to do it at a balanced pace, which was why the image feeds it provided of our enemy were so sporadic. If it had the energy to keep us abreast and collect the energy it needs to do whatever it's planning, it would've done so already."

Wa'raydon thought about what his mother said and glanced over at the –full symbiosis okay- question frantically flashing in his mind in.

"Something bad is coming and we are running out of time," he mumbled, feeling like something was squeezing his chest.

"Everything that's come has been bad, so something worse is coming," Adenetta said in cynical tone as she looked through the energy scope of her weapon, most likely scanning to see if there were any remaining enemy from the group of twenty or so Re'meka had just fired upon.

"How do you always know what G'o is doing? Are you in full symbiosis with it as well?" He asked his mother, trying to pull any bias from his tone as he watched the amber and red message change to all red.

A horn sounded again, and this time it was so loud he thought the building would crumble from the vibration alone. Inside the horn sound, he could make out something whistling. Knowing what the sound meant, it awoke a primal portion of himself that wanted nothing more than to survive.

"I accept full symbiosis G'o," he said telepathically as portions of the ceiling further down the chamber came crashing down.

"What's the point of worrying about life if I'm not going to give myself the best chance of having one," he reflected, feeling a gut-wrenching pain as G'o grew inside him.

The gut-wrenching pain quickly subsided, replaced by a feeling of indescribable pleasure.

"I can't even move. I feel like I'm high on U'nip weed," he thought, grinning ear-to-ear, feeling the gun slip out of his hand.

Soon the pleasurable sensation took on more of a tingling sensation wherever he had implant nodes. Giggling, he looked at the palms of his hand and watched as tiny green vines pushed his implants out.

"*Wow!*" He thought, finding the whole thing amusing, before starting to cough up blood with broken chunks of metal and plastic.

"Body map uploading: *Harmful implants removed. The metals and composites long-term effects on body would've been detrimental. Following implants with metals and crystals originating from Heka system, Kampana system, and planet Adrasteia. Still safe for use.*"

"I told him the implants the Void Force placed in him were cheap. All of the implants we gave him when he was an infant are still working," he heard his father mumble.

"Network connection established: *Rendezvous locations are as follows.*"

Wa'raydon could see map locations marked in green all over the planet. Next, he was able to see full images of the planet again, vice just outside images from G'o's point of view.

"Time reaming before last stand: *Seven minutes.*"

"Buffering relevant message traffic:"

Wa'raydon could hear men and women coordinating and encouraging others to get to locations near his mega building, which had been marked in green on the map he had seen moments before.

"Brain wave buffering complete. Thoughts are now shielded: *Your mathematical equations can be worked on with ninety percent safety.*"

"Multiple enemies incoming and present: *Proceeded to designated retreat location,*" flashed in his mind, with the image of a vine lined with thick sap running next to the building's lifts, which his parents had already been leading them towards.

As the merging effects wore off, he could hear the sound of the horn diminishing and as it did, images appeared in his mind showing him millions, if not more voidships launching into the air. At first he could only see human void spheres launching, but soon he could see voidships of every sort of sentient being living on the planet rising into the air.

From the human void spheres, he could see assault pods launching in every direction. From voidships resembling trees such as G'o, he could see large hexagonal spore-like pods bursting out of them, landing in the same locations as the human assault pods.

"Son, let's move!" His father shouted, tugging Adenetta.

The dust had cleared where the ceiling had collapsed and he could see men and women marching out in an odd grey-green battle armour he'd never seen before. As they formed up in rows and columns of one hundred, he took in the details of the world crest and unit symbols of Ah Tabai and thought, *"if they're Adrasteian sympathisers, then they're really going out of their way to trick people. If not, what gives? Why haven't they called out to us to see if we're okay?"*

Turning to ask Re'meka to see what she thought about them, he found her raising her weapon and taking aim. Then before he could even blink in surprise, she'd fired. With an almost silent whoosh, the explosive crystal orb hurtled into the group, turning the immediate seventeen people near its impact into broken chunks of armor and flesh. Then she was up, tugging his arm.

"Run! Sweetie!" She shouted, as a cascade of weapons fire erupted around them.

At one point, he felt his helmet forming, but not before he saw something flash against the right side of his eye. Even before he could come to terms with what the flash had meant, a mental image formed in his mind showing him that G'o was using a mixture of his body energy and its own to form temporary shields against laser and kinetic projectiles.

"So, I'm the reason why we've been moving so slow. If I'd said 'yes' to full symbiosis, we could've ran straight to this location. Instead, everyone has been moving slow, protecting me since I couldn't have taken the same amount of hits," he realised as they made it to the vine lined with thick sap.

His mother, Re'meka, then Adenetta, jumped into the vine.

"You're next son," his father said, sounding relieved.

"You go, you have my little sister on your back," he replied, pulling his father towards the vine, then pushing him into it.

Watching his father enter the vine, Wa'raydon felt his first moments of peace since the war had broken out.

"Locked in a life or death struggle with your family is unbearable. Every moment you wonder if they're going to die, how they're going to die or what to do if they die. And then, to find out that I was their biggest burden," he pondered sadly, waiting to get his first glimpse of the hexagonal spore-shaped pod that had crashed through the ceiling mere seconds after the human assault pod, wondering who or what would come out of it.

For the few seconds he waited, kinetic projectiles and laser fire hit his body shield, in which G'o promptly scolded him to take cover and completely form his helmet, explaining to him that the shielding technique wasn't one hundred percent.

"You know I hate the full helmet unless it's absolutely necessary, and nothing is one hundred percent," he muttered, watching the survivors of Re'meka's attack change direction of their fire to the spore-like pod opening out on all sides.

"Wow," he whispered, watching men and woman rush out of it with the likeness of his own organic metal armor, firing back on the men and woman wearing the insignia of Ah Tabai.

"Care to explain?" He asked G'o telepathically, stepping backwards till he slipped into the vine.

The moment he did, the rest of his helmet that hadn't come out when he'd taken the glancing blow against his body shield, extended out of the ports in his neck, wrapping fully around his head.

"Unbelievable," he thought, noticing the speed he descended down the vine was faster than if he were to freefall at terminal velocity.

"Enemy classification, Human: *Adrasteia Empire, Ah Tabai world government, Ah Tabaians controlled by non-humans, and advanced human civilizations with a multitude of agendas, known to your kind as 'Void Dwellers'.*"

Images of Adrasteians, Ah Tabaians and Ah Tabaians with organic metal armor appeared in his mind.

"I thought Void Dwellers are myths? What do they look like? I already know what the other three look like."

"Void Dwellers are real. There are several major Empires and several loosely founded civilizations. Your race has made a distinction between Empire and civilization by calling the loosely founded civilizations vagabonds of the void. While calling those who live in the void under one rule as Void Dweller. Essentially they're the same in terms of habitat preference. Stand by for visual."

Images of people appeared in his mind, but his mind couldn't comprehend what he was seeing.

"Her skin is translucent, and his is matte black, it doesn't even look like skin. And her hair resembles...fiber optics," he thought, already feeling overwhelmed with the sight of the Void Dweller people.

More images continued to flow past and the characteristics of the people continued to grow even stranger.

"All my enemies?" He asked, not understanding why so many advanced humans would want anything to do with his people.

"Yes, and no. To Void Dwellers, you're considered…an experiment. Some want results that would mean the survival of yourself and family, others want to see how you perish to test how much a person can take from whatever stressor they add into the environment. Whether they want you to live or die has nothing to do with what you would call 'good' or 'evil'. They only want their desired results in order to refine what they considered the 'Great Works'. However, there's no set group. All of their opinions wax and wane so you could never take comfort that any of the Void Dwellers have your best interest in mind. We must move on to non-human threats."

"Sure okay," he replied, wanting to know because of a sense of duty, but not really wanting to know because his spirit had already been crushed by the first group.

"Enemy classification, non-human: *Innumerable.*"

"Four non-human types are immediate threats: *Images of sentient beings are shown; however, you will not be able to tell who's your friend or foe from immediate observation. Will classify as encountered.*"

"This is your race and the other two I recognise. Both of them live in a sort of colonial symbioses with your kind. I've never seen any of you do anything harmful to people…but I guess not all of you are friendly huh?" He asked rhetorically.

"Much of my race and many others would like to make humans extinct."

"Kind of harsh…hey, what's the being that looks like a jelly fish? I've never seen this one."

"My race created them as bio-mechanical weapons; however, after billions of cycles they became sentient. Whenever there's a war between the races, they choose sides and jump in. Right now, many have chosen the side against humans for things your ancestors have done in the past and for what the Void Dwellers do on a consistent basis."

"Okay, why is all of this happening now? I just thought we're at war with Adrasteia and its sympathisers, now it seems like you're telling me everyone is the enemy. "

"Humans have a saying I will use."

"I'm listening."

"Phrase is…long story."

"You've got to be kidding me!" Wa'raydon shouted, unsure of why the answer amused him.

"So then, why are you helping us and all the others?"

"Why?"

"Yes, why?" He asked impatiently.

"What's your favorite thing to do Wa'raydon?"

He was taken aback by the simplicity of the question and by the subject change, but his mind instantly thought of making love, eating, and then taking a one person void sphere into the void for a few hours before returning home and repeating the cycle all over again.

"Exactly," G'o said in his mind.

"Exactly?" Wa'raydon repeated.

"There are billions of people who think just like you, and millions have lived inside of my body. What harm do people with your mindsets pose to anyone or anything? None. So why should I be biased, angry, or vengeful to people such as yourself," G'o responded.

"I see," Wa'raydon replied, understanding completely.

"So tell me this, are you male or female? When you speak, it's smooth and soothing. Yet I cannot say I know your voice."

"I function as a tree, neither male nor female. I have both parts for reproduction. I speak using electromagnetic transmissions directly to your mind. One day you'll be able to hear the difference in the transmissions more clearly, then you'll be able to distinguish the voices of my race and many others, even as we speak to each other across the void."

"I hope I live that long," he replied darkly, then asked, "So you're a tree?"

"No."

"What?"

"Long story."

"That's a human expression, I'm banning you from using it."

"Humans weren't around for trillions galactic cycles. Using your logic, then I ban you from using the phrase. And your race from existing."

"Hey not funny! Wait, trillions of…?"

"Drink deeply for the spore symbiosis to take effect."

"What?" Wa'raydon asked as he flew out of the vine.

By the time he'd gotten his bearings, his body hit the most crystal clear water he'd ever seen in his life. As he surfaced, his armor retracted and the water instantly began to dig into his body, reminding him of a deep tissue massage. Remembering what G'o had instructed, he opened his mouth and took long gulps of water.

"*WOW!*" He thought, feeling refreshed and his stomach knocking all in one.

"Took you long enough!" He heard as he swam to the shore.

"I wanted to see something," he replied to his mother, running to the nearest covering of plant growth, popping a squat.

"Your body is getting rid of the rest of the cheap hardware the government put in your body. Even after hundreds of cycles of scalding from billions of people like myself, they never took the time to invest in stealth trade ships or able personnel to acquire useful material the roundabout way. If they did, we would've been able to acquire way more substantive levels of Heka system metals and Kampana system crystals from the Empires and civilization that trade with Adrasteia.

"Uhhh, okay, can we talk about this in a moment? My stomach is killing me," he said, feeling the broken chunks of material as they made their way through his intestine.

"Acquiring planet Adrasteia's crystals and metals are of course a whole other story. In terms of trade, no one can get their hands on them since Blood Empress Dakini always ensures every microgram is accounted for and put to use. Unfortunately, the only time you'd see that kind of material from there is when someone's trying to either shoot you dead or run you through," his mother said, appearing from around his plant cover to stand in front of him.

"MOM!?"

"What? Is it not coming out? Breath baby, squeeze your tummy."

"Really!? Go away!"

"No, hurry up. And you should be asking why."

"Mom, WHY! Are you standing here!?"

"So you'll hurry up. So your question is - why are some foreign bodies vehemently rejected from my body while others are not? That's a good question son."

"Go away, go away, go away."

"The reason human bodies don't reject materials from those two systems or from planet Adrasteia is twofold. First, they're forms of life even though they're not alive exactly. The Adrasteia Empire calls them helix-materials because every last one of them has a helix structure. Some are simple single helix structures, others are in complex forms I still find hard to believe.

Which brings me to the second reason. Humans are inherently good at understanding the layers of knowledge required to mix and meld the helix-materials. Meaning we can use helix-materials in any form of alchemy we choose, whether it be body alchemy or with machines. For instance, just before you were born, we hired some void pirates to get us any kind of helix-material they could get their hands on. They came back with eight forms of crystal and eight forms of metal, and each material was octuple helix in nature. Neither one of us had ever seen or worked with them before, yet it was easy for us to craft your birth implants to fit your body."

"Really! You two hired void pir….uhhh. Sounds interesting, love you, thank you for taking good care of me."

"Love you too son. So if you're confused at the concept of these metals and crystals being organic like, consider oil. Oil is an organic based material made from billions of cycles of dead leaves, animals, and so on, which are then compressed underground and after alchemic process, it's then created. The metals and crystals are made similarly to how oil is formed. Their origins are from animals and beings whose bodies were made of organic metal and crystal who've died, and after billions if not more cycles of alchemic processes underground, have become what they are today."

"Yhea, like I said, really amazing," Wa'raydon said, picturing everything in his mind now that he'd finished relieving himself.

Hopping up, he practically ran to the water, and after washing himself, he came out and made sure he made eye contact with everyone.

"I'm sorry, I was being selfish. I had no idea I was the biggest burden."

"You weren't a burden," Adenetta said reassuringly.

"I was definitely a burden. Mom was even pretending she was having difficulty with the feed from G'o earlier," he replied quickly.

"Okay in one sense, but it's a big decision you had to make in very little time. G'o approached us with this right after you left on deployment. And I said no all the way up until those very suggestive commercials came on."

"Last stand: *Stand by,*" flashed before his eyes.

Suddenly the underground chamber illuminated by G'o went dark. Then the pool of water in front of them began to crackle with electric arcs in arrays of color he'd never seen before.

"Three Adrasteian armadas located. Prioritising attack by system location and armada size: *R'yu system, one. Yin't & Yin'n, two. Adrasteia outer orbit, three.*"

"Entanglement points open: *Firing.*"

Wa'raydon's mouth opened in shock watching three golden orbs the size of his fist form over the water. When they were as bright as the blue star of Adrasteia binary, they simultaneously dropped into the water then vanished along with all the water.

"I never thought I'd live to see another being open up entanglement points with its body energy, let alone carry out a three prong attack while doing so," his father said sounding awestruck.

Wa'raydon could feel the last of G'o major presence disappear. Taking its place he could now feel the personality of the being that had been planted within him when he had first come out of the cocoon.

"Hi, I am R'o, it's dark, you need light… and we should go meet the others."

"Sure," Wa'raydon muttered sarcastically as his vison adjusted and a visual indicator pointed him in the direction of the rendezvous location.

Turning around, he smiled at his family, feeling an odd sense of safety knowing that G'o had just carried out attack against Adrasteia. The looks on their faces showed that none shared his sentiment.

"Isn't what just happened good news?" He asked, walking backwards to still see their faces.

"Son its targets weren't on this planet. Why do you think that is?" His mother asked in a reprimanding tone.

"The main threat is obviously Adrasteia," he replied, feeling his mind starting to slip into auto math mode in which everywhere he looked, his mind would do calculations of angles, thickness, and dimensions.

"Innocent to the core. That's why we love him," Re'meka said dourly.

"It means this place is lost, our love," Adenetta whispered.

"Then why attack Adrasteia, when…?" Wa'raydon stopped talking, visualising what was going on outside.

"Oh crap," he muttered, following his families chain of thought.

"What?" Adenetta asked.

"No I get it now. It was right before my eyes. Everyone's biggest threat would be Adrasteia coming to the moon-worlds indiscriminately wiping out all life. Which is why there are so many sentient beings leaving the planet right now. G'o's attack is just to buy time for his race and all of the others to get off the moon-worlds and most likely away from this binary system."

"Correct, and we better hope we can get off of Ah Tabai as well. The attack G'o carried out can take a few days or even up to a month to reach the armadas. If it's the latter, the armadas will have grown to a point where the attacks may barely make a dent in their man power," his father said.

"Why a few days?! Or even a month?! Entanglement points are always instant unless you're near strong dimensional anomalies. I definitely know all about this!" Wa'raydon shouted defensively, not wanting to be lectured on something he was always top in the class for.

"You know all there is to know about the use of machines using metal and crystal to entangle locations. You can do the math and operate said machinery to create those points with your voidships. How long does it take to create a stable point for an armada?" His father probed calmly.

"Four days. But if you do cluster points, it'll take only two. And you can even honeycomb entanglement points and come out like hornets from a hive." Wa'raydon said pridefully.

"How long does it take for a living being to create an entanglement point?" His mother chimed in.

"I don't know, but G'o said entanglement points open, not creating, meaning they were already there! And I could feel that prickly feeling all over my body. They were fully formed, not being created!" He shouted, growing even more annoyed, priding himself on the fact that he knew what entanglement points felt like.

"Okay fine, say you're right and they were already formed. Now where does the attack come out? An already created point at the target location? The Adrasteian's aren't going to hang out in front of random pre-formed entanglement points, waiting to see what comes out of it.

Those people are many things, unfortunately one of the things they're not, is dumb in warfare tactics. They'd never even rest in front of their own points in fear of being attacked," his father said, kissing his mother on the side of the head.

"Oh no!" Wa'raydon screamed, taking off running at breakneck speed, leaving his family behind.

"Hey! Hey! What! What?" Re'meka screamed.

"We are!" He replied, running even faster to the rendezvous point.

"We are what?" His father screamed.

"The moon-worlds affiliation guarding the two thousand entanglement points are just waiting around to get attacked!" He screamed.

"Son, it's not the same! Adrasteia would need a multi-billion, if not more warheads to pull of an attack on the blockades," his mother shouted as he made it to a tunnel bathed in luminous green light.

"I never said Adrasteia!" He screamed, running faster.

R'o had shown him the mathematical equations behind G'o's entanglement points during his argument with is parents. He could see that G'o had targeted the Adrasteian armadas by isolating entangled atom pairs that were on Ah Tabai and the Adrasteian voidships.

The entanglements between the atoms weren't strong enough to make two transit points, so G'o oscillated the atoms on the Adrasteian voidships while sending its attack through the first points to wait in limbo. The oscillation G'o created on the atoms of the voidships would then cause all the atoms around them to harmonize, creating the end transit point which would appear directly on the Adrasteian voidships.

After understanding this, Wa'raydon could see why his father had said it'd take a few days or possibly up to a month, but that's not what had freaked him out. After he had completed the mathematical equations R'o had shown him, he was able to see something he was sure his parents and many others hadn't considered. Which was the manner in which G'o was able to isolate the entangled atoms in the first place.

"There are more than one pair of entangled atoms everywhere!? There are multiple entangled pairs! How many entanglement pairs can there be at any given time? If what I just calculated is correct, there can be entangled atoms pairs across the known universe. Not only that, but G'o could intuitively sense which ones were connected and instantly grab hold of them. That's the difference between a living being and a machine," he reflected, opening a channel to the rendezvous location.

"Hey, this is Tier four, Void Assault Admiral Wa'raydon. Do you have any channels that work off world?"

"All off world networks are down, we've never seen anything like this. The entanglement crystals connected to the receivers and transmitters are fully operational. It makes no sense," a woman replied.

"Ah! Damn it! It's way too late!" He bellowed, slowing down and finally stopping his mad dash.

When his family caught up, they bombarded him with questions he couldn't even hear as he visualised what was happening at every single one of the two thousand blockade points, which at minimum was surrounded by five hundred thousand void spheres.

"Hey, care to explain son? We know you're slow till you're fast. And when your brain is finally working, everyone else needs to be filled in," his father said sounding semi-serious.

"G'o showed me all of our enemies as I came down the vine. He showed me that many of its race don't like us. Well guess what? They played us! They let us do all the entanglement point linking for them. All of them can feel multiple entangled atom pairs, and instantly collect and manipulate them with their body energy. And unlike our own body energy that ends just past arms reach unless we force it to extend further, theirs naturally stretches far out into the void.

All they have to do is find the atoms connected to every intra-ship link, intra-planetary radio, or our own entanglement points. Which is what they're doing now. That's why intra-planetary radios and intra-ship links aren't working! Seven lives! If that's not bad enough, I'm even more certain that entanglement transit for most humans in this binary system isn't working!"

"Yhea, but there are a few like G'o who are using the ent...," his father began to say, but Wa'raydon knew what he was going to say and cut him off.

"And I'm willing to bet my remaining six lives, there are way more who hate us than like us going through them, because if I were a human sympathiser, I'd be getting far away from this solar system, not going to any of the other moon-worlds to bunker down or rescue others. And they definitely wouldn't enter into the midst of the armed blockades."

Seeing the look on his parents' faces, he could tell after all they'd been through, this time they really did seem surprised.

"So you two don't know everything, huh? A little while ago I had asked G'o why all of this is happening now, and it said long story. How about you two finally giving me a straight answer? Why is all of this insanity happening now?"

His mother's green blue eyes lit up with what he believed was an idea, but her warm honey-brown face took on a red hue which puzzled him, causing him to wonder what in the seven lives would cause her to feel embarrassed.

"Remember we had asked you if your armada had come close to any of the blocked entanglement points or if you knew of anyone in your fleet trying to secretly meet someone from the Heka system?

"Yes, I remember."

"There are people called the Niya who were once a very powerful Empire, boosting around ten trillion people. Sixty cycles ago, Adrasteia's Empress rescued the very last of them from annihilation from beings like G'o. The seventeen billion that remained were then granted refuge by her and have lived pretty much evenly distributed throughout the forty six moon-worlds of Heka.

You would've never heard about this if it weren't for a time like this. Speaking about the rescue of the Niya is forbidden and punishable by death on all the free moon-worlds of Adrasteia binary. I think this situation was the very first time all the moon-world governments were finally able to agree unanimously on one thing, which is to make sure Empress Dakini is always seen in a negative light."

"You've got to be kidding me. So people here knew the danger and did nothing?" He asked, glaring at Adenetta and Re'meka to see if they were as lost as he was.

Seeing that they were, he looked back at his parents, shaking his head in disbelief.

"And remember I was just lecturing you about humans inherently knowing how to use the helix-materials?" His mother asked, sounding slightly nervous.

"How could I forget?"

"Well long story short is that there've been a few alchemic understanding breakthroughs in regards to these materials in the last five cycles. The most recent breakthroughs were made by a team of Niya scientists that secretly share information with special contacts on the free moon-worlds, hoping either Adrasteia or people from the free moon-worlds use these advancements to harm or wipe out the beings that almost wiped them out."

"Well that makes sense because…"

"G'o's race rely heavily on symbioses with other sentient beings my love. If we humans weren't a nuisance to sentient beings in this system before, we are now a very viable threat. And it's not just to beings in this system, but to any in arms reach of the Adrasteia Empire. And from what your father and I know, and what G'o knew when it attacked those three armadas, is that Adrasteia has already planned down to the smallest detail, the genocide of G'o's entire race, with their secondary goal being the annihilation of any race associated with them. Which truth be told, is ninety-five percent of all the sentient beings living within this dwarf Galaxy.

Chapter IX

Awaking refreshed in darkness

Two days later

**Location: R'yu solar system, aboard Tier five
Admiral Sandreaka's main void sphere 'Voice of Kali'**

**Void Crew under Sandreaka's direct command:
One million**

**Voidship's current population:
Approximately three point five million**

BANDARES EYES OPENED AND BEFORE he had a chance to think, he felt something poking his toes and knees. Looking down, he saw Lolina smiling up at him, jabbing him with something sharp.

"How do you feel?" She asked, still grinning at him.

"I really don't know what to say. I've never felt this good before to put a name to it," he said, flexing and twisting his body, taking advantage of the free range of motion he was allowed while hovering in the levitation beam.

"Good to hear. So let's review a few important things now that you feel good to go," Lolina said, giving him a brighter smile than she had before.

"Tier three, Ground Assault Elite General Lolina, aka 'Ice doctor'. Favorite food: anything candy. Favorite sport: sleeping. Favorite position: a person's tongue. Hummm, before all I saw was your name and title. Now I can see your full bio, which seems to be filled with only sarcastic answers," he said, smiling as he read more of her bio.

"You're Ground Assault Elite as well now," she responded, changing parts of her bio to read even more absurd things as she released him from the levitation beam.

Stepping down from the beam's platform, he knelt down and kissed her booted feet.

"Thank you for taking care of me," he said, before standing up.

"You're as short as Tara and I," she replied teasingly.

"Ahh! Back to being mean to me I see. I am of your will," he retorted sarcastically, slightly bowing.

"Oh! No! By the Empress, stop that right now! Okay, Okay, I get the point, stand straight and listen up. You're fully upgraded with all the latest and greatest the Empire has to offer. In your right hand, there's an unformed trident; in your left, I gave you a special shield. The physical properties of the shield are a variation of crystal lined with metal, which combined is only a nanometer thick.

This alone can stop almost any fast-moving kinetic projectile or energy beam. On top of that, the shield has an energy barrier that is sourced from both ambient energy and your body energy. The more energy striking the shield, the greater it repulses."

"So, I'm indestructible?" He asked jokingly, hoping she'd say yes.

"Yes, if we're talking about most human or sentient being Tier one civilizations or Empires. If you have to fight trained human alchemist or worse trained sentient being alchemist from civilizations or Empires who are on the cusp of Tier two like ourselves, not a chance.

So, before you try to become a one person army, you'll need to learn how to fight alongside your peers. On that note, you'll be meeting your squad leader very shortly and she's perfect for training you in your type of fighting style."

"My type of fighting style?" Bandares repeated, trying to recall if he did anything special during combat training that could constitute as having a style.

"Yes, you're an intimate fighter. Up close and personal. Remember, I was there when you fought T'mot. You could've fought him by throwing something at him, like the medical kit or one of the many benches. But you moved to him and connected your punches."

"Yhea, but everyone does that in a fight, no?"

"Yes and no, mostly not. That's why people make guns and bombs. People want to disconnect from the harm they cause. During your lifetime as a solider, you'll see how many people want death and harm to come to people, yet hide behind the button or the long throw,

hoping they'd never need to go near the bodies after the deed is done."

"I don't understand, T'mot fought me in the same fashion—kicking and punching. How is he different than I?" Bandares asked, feeling like they were having two different conversations.

Lolina's eyes seemed to glaze over and Bandares couldn't tell if she was thinking of an answer to his question or having a mental conversation.

"Bandares, everyone in our brigade can be considered an intimate fighter. It's why we have been chosen as Elite. But you show a distinct preference for this type of fighting and you have the worst scores for shooting I've ever seen in my life. Granted back then your implants weren't helping you aim, so you were at a disadvantage. Maybe because of that disadvantage, your hand-to-hand abilities evolved the way they did. That's good. You overcame your shortcomings and have inadvertently developed some very unique abilities that Tara and I rarely see. Now form your trident."

Bandares brought up his right hand and looked into his palm.

"Interesting," he said under his breath, tracing the red-yellow metal and dark red crystal lines that ran alongside his veins.

"Doesn't look like a lot of metal or crystal right? It's one of the many properties that makes the helix-materials so remarkable. By their very nature they're already compact, yet extremely bountiful. The materials I put in your hand are in single helix form. This way you can use basic alchemy skills to begin personalizing the materials by adding portions of your DNA or any other helix-materials you think would work well within the composite structures."

Bandares sent a command to his hand and watched the red-yellow trace lines disintegrate then rise from his hand, forming into an orb which hovered about an inch above his palm.

"Move your head back, it prevents itself from forming into its overly curious owners," Lolina said, sounding like she was forcing herself not to laugh at his ignorance.

Moving his head back and his hand outwards, the orb moved outward diagonally. Then in a movement faster than his eyes could track, it formed into trident.

"It hovers off the ground?" He asked rhetorically as he took in the details of the eerie red-yellow metallic staff containing three dark red crystal points at the forward end and one dark red crystal point at the bottom.

"Yes of course, all Imperial weapons are telekinetically linked to the owner. Right now, this is its default form. The easiest way for a beginner like you to personalise it a bit more is to play around with the preprogramed settings till you find something you like.

As your alchemy skills grow, you'd be able to change the properties of the materials as you like, but you have to be careful doing that or you can build your weapon with detrimental flaws. Oh, and you can even choose to turn it into a single point spear or sword, as some people find the idea of a trident a bit awkward."

"Can I choose not to use it?" Bandares asked, not knowing what to think about using any form of weapon.

"Sure. After you become a Tier three like me you can. For now, you need to learn how to use one or all three of the traditional weapons, both in combat and how to personalise it using alchemy. Trust me, always using and growing with one or changing use between all three of them till you become Tier three pays off.

If you choose not to use one of the three basic weapons later on, it's most likely because you'd have found a weapon that really works with your personality. Like me, I use these," Lolina said, producing six silver hand-axes that floated in front of their faces.

The blades along with the bottom of the handgrip were made of dark blue crystal and he noticed he couldn't see where the head of the axe connected with the handgrip.

"How's that work?" He asked, pointing to the gap, "and how'd you call these out so fast? And from where?"

"Entanglement magnetism. The gap is perfect for all sorts of things, such as swinging down at an enemy, then only moving the axe head for a kill strike, or for implanting various enhancements such as crystals, metals, and various forms of energy. My personal favorite is a mixture of all three. Then, when I throw it or jam it into an enemy with a special shield such as your own, it'll behave as a personalized bomb to take it down. Understand? And the answer to where they came from or how fast I was able to summon them, is my secret."

"Yhea, I understand, you dream of bombing me and you have a secret axe hiding places in the middle of the air," he mumbled, recalling his trident into his hand while calling up the stats and specs of the helix-materials placed within his body that would serve as both his battle armor and space suit.

"Oh, I can personalise my armor?"

"Yup. There are two reasons you're seeing a lot of generic armor with standard Imperial crest and what not. One, is because they're rookies. Two, because people like me don't show their real body armor unless it's a fight worth calling it out for. It's obvious we're not all friends here, so why let people study your armor. When and if they see what you've got, it should be just before you kill them."

"Okay, I'm getting scalded for keeping you here. Go meet your squad leader and the rest of your team. Your implants will guide you."

Bandares bowed deeply and just as he was about to utter words of endearment, he felt her hand pushing on his head.

"Out you go," she giggled, pushing him all the way out the medical chamber while he remained in his bowing position.

Standing up straight, he saw her smiling and shaking her head as the blast door closed.

"Out of the way sex toy," he heard, just as something hard slammed into his chest.

Without thinking, he formed his armor around his nude body.

"What'd you say!?" He growled, turning and grabbing the man's left arm, pulling it down and outward as hard as he could.

The man was muscular and already armored, standing six feet seven to his five foot one, but the way he pulled the man's arm instantly made him lose his balance.

"AHHrguh!" The man bellowed as his head swung toward the blast door of the medical chamber.

Before the man's head hit the blast door, it opened, sending him flailing through, almost crashing into Lolina who'd nimbly stepped out of the way.

"Sex toy huh?" Bandares asked, feeling a fire inside of his stomach as he lunged into the medical chamber after the man.

"You think, I'll allow it!?" He asked in a snarl, kicking the man on the ass with his armored foot.

Assuming the man didn't feel too much from the impact due to his own armor, Bandares called out his trident and mentally commanded it to impale the man in the thighs. Seeing the points of his trident drive into the man with ease, he felt a calmness overcome him that left him almost breathless. For a long moment he opted to simply watch as the man wailed and screamed, awkwardly reaching back trying to fully wrap one of his hands around the trident in a feeble attempt to pull it out.

"Don't touch it!" Bandares roared, now feeling fully empower by the man's sobs.

Kicking the man's hands off the trident, he snarled "tell everyone in your brigade if they ever, even have a wet dream of touching me again! I'll impale their assholes in their sleep as the closing to their dream! Is that clear!?"

"Clearrr…Its clearrr!" The man wailed louder, giving Bandares a feeling of pure domineering satisfaction that bordered on hysterical joy.

Taking deep breaths, Bandares took a few steps back and then with his mind, he raised the trident out of the man's thighs, then moved it towards his head.

"Crawl out… and do not look at me or my Tier three General. If you do, the points will find their way through the back of your head, into your eyes."

"Wait! I wonder if he is one of them," he thought, watching the man begin to slow crawl towards the blast door.

Kicking the man to make him pause, he came around and looked at his face to see if he remembered him standing in front of his stasis pod.

"Lucky," he mumbled moving behind him, then kicking him again, this time right up the center of his crotch, letting him know he wanted him to continue his crawl.

When the man made it through the blast door, Bandares spit on the trail of blood he'd left behind, hoping that was a strong enough gesture to curse the man's blood and stifle his healing.

"Well then, looks like you're a natural at telekinesis. And it looks like I did a good job forming the tips to your trident. They went through his armor like butter and trust me his armor would normally deflected such a basic attack. I must say, the new pre-made helix-material composites the Niya woman gave Tara to distribute throughout the brigade are already paying off. I honestly wouldn't have thought of that kind of tip design until I saw how the materials were layered," Lolina said with a wide grin on her face, appearing totally un-phased by the entire episode.

Bandares heard what she'd said and many questions filled his mind, but they were quickly smothered out by a deep sense of shame.

"I apologise," he stammered, staring at his saliva mixed with blood, wondering when he'd become so feral.

"For taking vengeance? Why?"

"Because I lost my temper. I don't know what came over me. But it felt so good."

"Yup, that's why there are terms like vengeance is sweet. Speaking of which, I forgot to tell you, you're now hosting. It's not brain worms though. Your body wouldn't accept them. So I engineered a type of wart virus that lives in your body, but won't really harm you. You may have a mild outbreak here and there, but nothing more. I guarantee if anyone ever gets to you again, they'll wish on all seven lives and both Goddesses, they hadn't. All the fine details are in your files marked 'must review'. Now get out, I want some alone time, I've already spent enough time with you and that other pain in the ass Yon'tu," Lolina said, pulling him and pushing him through the blast door.

"Who did this to you?" He heard a woman say as she lifted up the man he'd impaled.

He could see the man's armor had closed and had most likely stopped the bleeding. Looking at the woman's armor, he could see she was also from the man's brigade and felt another burst of unchecked rage. Without even thinking about it, he shoved both of them as hard as he could, making them topple over in front of him. As the woman floundered underneath the man, Bandares stepped on her stomach armor, then stepped over her face. As he did, he said, "I did," in the most casual tone he could muster, hoping it added even more insult to his actions.

"Bandares, my name is Anahita, your Tier two squad leader. Get your ass here now," Anahita said in his mind.

"Yes, squad leader," he replied, starting to jog as he called up the meeting location.

"I wonder how Tara is doing. If I try to speak with her, will she be upset? She has thousands of people to deal with. I'm just one of them," he thought, calling up her location.

"Everything I think, my implants automatically do for me. And this time it's not overwhelming me! I see! I was missing out on a lot!" Bandares realised, calling up functions of his implants.

"You can test your implants when you're here. Run faster," Anahita said impatiently in his mind.

"Invasive isn't she!?" He thought, picking up the pace, making it to the chamber in a minute and a half's time.

"Welcome, I'm glad you finally made it here. We have a lot to cover, and very little time," Anahita said, giving him an awkward smile.

"She doesn't look like how she sounds," he thought doing a double take, taking in the details of her slender frame, with high cheek bones and long, straight black hair that reached the floor.

He could hear scoffs and jokes from familiar voices that made him cringe. Shifting his gaze, he saw T'mot, Ve'sops, and Po'be first. Behind them, he saw Yon'tu, who as usual, kept himself near but not too close to anyone else. Studying Yon'tu further, it seemed to him as if Yon'tu were inside of his own head searching or reading something from his implants.

"Short, but cute," a woman exclaimed as he felt something tap against the armour around his buttocks.

Startled by the voice, he turned to see group of women he had walked past without noticing and almost panicked.

"My apologies, I didn't see any of you," he said, unconsciously making a head count of five women.

"Form up! Bandares, Yon'tu, Nana, Me'na, Jov'na. You five stand here in this sacred geometric. T'mot, Ve'sops, Po'be, Keshena, and Cassia. In this geometric here. This is your standard battle formation. Your entire universe for now on, consist of the twist, swirls, and connecting points of the geometrics you now stand within."

Bandares looked down at the complexity of the geometric and felt overwhelmed. He also felt a little self-conscious of where he stood, wondering if she wanted him to stand in a specific location within the sacred geometric.

"Notice I didn't tell any of you were to stand? That's because you need to see, and I need to see where you place yourselves in relation to each other, and within the geometric. This will tell you your team dynamics. Take a look at each other and see what you can glean from your body positions and report to me what you think. I'll give you a few minutes to ponder. Also during this time I want only the men to call in their body armor, this will help you connect with the sacred geometric as you formulate your responses," Anahita said as she walked towards the chamber blast door, just as an older woman with somewhat similar facial features came through it.

Calling in his armour, he watched Anahita bow deeply, then point to him and next to Yon'tu. Then both Anahita and the woman walked back to the original position she'd been standing when he'd first arrived.

"Bandares, I see you looking at me? Do you already have an answer or are you fantasizing about me?" Anahita asked in a flat tone.

Bandares hadn't even thought of her in that way until she'd mentioned it. He'd been too preoccupied trying to figure out why the older woman exuded such a warm, loving feeling. From the moment she'd walked into the chamber, her presence reminded him of his mother, holding him just before she passed away from 'The Grey', a disease that turned a person to skin and bone, with rotting grey flesh all within the time frame of a single day.

'I feel like I could run to her arms, and tell her my every desire and all of my secrets,' he mused, staring fixedly at the woman.

"Fantasizing about me it is. If you really need sex, come to me after the lesson. In normal circumstances however, whenever you need sex, come to me or your female peers before the lesson. I don't want any more day dreaming and fantasizing from you. All those fun thoughts should be taken out on us so that you're one hundred percent focused and combat ready when I begin my lessons. Is that clear Bandares?"

"What'd she just say!? Just go ask her or the other women for sex? No intimacy, no flirting, she offers sex like it's just duty? What kind of culture is this? Tara told me I'd see subtle changes in social dynamics. This isn't subtle," he thought, feeling his body grow warm as he stuttered, "Cla-cla-cla-clear, squad leader!"

"All of us are going to be working really close together, through some real messed up situations that I plan for us not to die in. So what I just said to Bandares goes for the rest of you men as well. I can't afford for any of you to be wondering what our kunusses smell, taste, or feel like. Or what interesting moves we can do. People who've kept those natural and normal thoughts bottled up in their heads, have died and gotten those people they were day dreaming about killed.

All because they were too caught up in lustful fantasies during training and briefs, failing to hear that the enemy had special weapons that could smash through their shields or armor and so on and so forth. And yes, I said people, not just men, so when we need you men for our fantasies, we're coming straight to all of you as well. Bandares, why do you look so confused?"

"Well, I thought that women only want men for reproduction and that any pleasure women receive from the act, is only in that context. We were always told that when women desire physical pleasure, they seek that among themselves."

"Whatever you thought or are thinking right now is dead wrong. You still have the mindset of a slave and need to let go of that mental repression. The only part you got right is the last part and that's only to a certain extent. In terms of women wanting men for just pleasure without the duty of making a child. Of course we want that Bandares, forever embed that in your brain. As a matter of fact, many women in this brigade want the same amount of physical attention from men as men want from women.

If we're talking about the women in this particular squad, it's always way more. On that note, after this lesson, we'll have a group love making session to start building all of your stamina and imaginations to our levels. When we're all trapped on some stupid planet we're ordered to besiege, we ladies don't want to be bored and stuck with no recreation, all because you five start cumming too fast without knowing how to recover."

Bandares heard some of the women snicker in agreement and felt his kudock starting to grow in anticipation.

"You're the one distracting me! Before, I was fine. Now, all I can think about is kunuss!" He thought, wishing the brief would end already, but his lust was short lived when he heard T'mot whisper, "we're wasting valuable lesson time teaching dumbass Bandares common sense."

"I didn't want to say anything, but the stamina training is mostly for you. Lolina said that on your first go, you only lasted fifteen seconds. That's pretty bad, even for a virgin, but I think she was more upset you got sleepy and wanted to cuddle right after," Anahita said without missing a beat, drawing out soft chuckles from the women.

Looking over in T'mot direction, he could see that T'mot and his crew all had their eyes fixed firmly on the ground in shame and thought.

"Finally someone can shut you up!"

"Bandares, don't smile too hard, you'll hurt your cheeks. Nope, that evil smirk you're making isn't any better, it'll give you face wrinkles. Anyways, now that I've cleared up that whole fantasy situation, let's get back to the main lesson. Does anyone have an answer to my question about where you have placed yourself inside the sacred geometrics?

In addition to that question, have any of you figured out what some of the patterns mean? Nana, put your hand down. Anyone male, who hasn't been with the brigade since its founding, have an answer?" Anahita asked, looking first to Yon'tu then over to T'mot and the rest, which gave Bandares a moment to breathe feeling her attention had been taken off him.

"No one? Well that's disappointing, I was hoping someone would have an intuitive, gut-feeling answer. All of you now have the title of Elite after all, I was assuming your instincts would be sharper," Anahita said, shaking her head in what Bandares considered to be a mock display of disappointment.

"Squad leader?" T'mot piped up cockily, seeming to have already regained his self-esteem, causing Bandares left eye to twitch.

"I bet one of my seven lives he wants to reopen the topic about sex because he knows I'm still a virgin and wants to fling it in my face to make himself feel better," he thought.

"Yes T'mot, you have an answer?"

"Umm. No, I was hoping you could help me understand a few things. If that's okay with you of course?"

"I don't like tangents, will this help you answer my question?"

"I don't...umm. I'm afraid it might be a tangent," T'mot replied nervously.

Bandares saw the older women whisper something to Anahita, then smile. From the look on Anahita's face he could tell she didn't like whatever the woman had said.

"This is Lanying of the Niya people. She's here to discuss the enemy we'll face in great detail. She says that in her wisdom, tangents are also forms of direct lines to truths and answers of clarity. So, what's your question or questions, T'mot?"

"Thank you, squad leader and Lanying. Well, my question comes as former squad leader."

Bandares felt so annoyed the moment T'mot said that, he didn't even hear the rest of what he had to say. In the end, all he heard was laughter. Looking up, he could see Anahita and Lanying's faces glowing bright red. And to him, it seemed like they were doing everything in their power not to double over in laughter.

Taking deep breaths to calm himself, Bandares stared at the curved line he stood on, tracing it to Yon'tu, who he could see was tracing the same line back to him. When their eyes met, Yon'tu smirked and bobbed his head, then looked away towards another set of patterns on the geometric.

"From the lessons I learned in my sleep, this is a pattern for energy flow. What's this line represent again? Oh yes, synergy! And this curved portion with a point is a symbol of a pointed shield. Aimed at...T'mot."

Bandares turned around and followed a twisted line, with a straight line running through it to the woman closest to him. Looking up at her, she turned her attention away from T'mot and flashed him a mischievous smile as she made it obvious she was checking out his kudock.

"Tier two, Ground Assault Elite Nana, second in command of this squad. Her bio says she's a perfectionist that fights with gruesome tactics, yet she's extremely loving and extremely sensual. It also says she's in charge of an infiltrator unit. I wonder how being in two squads work out?" He thought as he closed her bio and took in the details of the slender woman standing before him.

Catching his eyes traveling up her body, she did a slow seductive hip wind that instantly made him look to her face. The moment he did, she tilted her head towards a location on the geometric to her right, containing a round curve and sharp pointed edge that was also aimed at T'mot.

"Another pointed shield aimed at T'mot. So, I'm not the only one wary of him," he thought, feeling oddly relieved as he nodded his thanks to Nana.

Seeing him nod, she then tilted her head towards a group of long, thick, smooth lines to her left, which connected her location to the other two women who stood in the geometric. When he looked at the lines as a whole, he could see that as they reached each woman they'd form a perfect circle around them.

"Each woman stands within a perfect circle, with thick interconnected lines smoothly going to each other. I think this symbolizes unity, trust, and deep friendship, yet demarked by strong individuality, which is shown by the space within the perfect circles," his gut feeling told him.

With that thought, he felt someone staring at the back of his neck, which made him turn to look at Anahita and then to Lanying. Although both women were still chuckling and still facing T'mot's direction, with Anahita's mouth still moving as she answered T'mot's questions, he could still feel both women's full attention aimed solely on him.

"And that's why a squad of slaves consist roughly of one thousand people, while a brigade squad roughly consist of ten people, plus the leader," Bandares managed to hear Anahita say.

"Oh, I see. And, squad leader? Surely we cannot all be Elite. I mean some are stronger than others. What constitutes one being considered Elite? Where did this wonderful title come from?" T'mot asked, in which Bandares could feel T'mot's eyes boring into the side of his face.

"Well we'll find out now, T'mot…we'll find out right now," Anahita said, waving her hand.

Bandares didn't even understand what had happened, all he could tell was that he was weightlessly tumbling end-over-end. Less than a second later, all he could see was pure darkness. Unable to hear any sound or breathe any air, the only presence he could perceive as he tumbled was the even darker than void, orb silhouette of the main voidship, which his implants labeled 'Voice of Kali' every time his eyes fell upon it as he continued his wild flips in the void.

"This is what it's like to be ambushed and blown into the void. The Elite will survive and return with an answer to my questions," Anahita said in his mind.

Feeling his protective implants kicking in, even before his armor had a chance to wrap around his body, Bandares began to smile and thought.

"I never thought tumbling in darkness, with no air to breath and where no one can see my face, is where I'd feel the most alive and free!"

Chapter X

Development of an Individual

TARA STOOD NERVOUSLY OUTSIDE THE airlock waiting for the all clear. When the blue light flicked on, she rushed in just in time to see Anahita, Lanying, and the other women retracting their helmets into their bodies.

"Blue star, how are you?" Anahita inquired, giving her a knowing look.

"I'd be better when he get his ass back in the voidship," she replied frankly, searching the women's faces for signs of humor, and seeing none.

"Humph! I expected at least one of you to call me out on having a crush on a rookie!" She exclaimed, completely serious.

"Actually, if you won't take his virginity, I will. I like the darkness inside him. He reminds me of felines who live in prides, warm and sweet with its own but will kill something without regard,"

"Are you challenging me?" Tara growled, stepping directly into Anahita's face.

"I hardly think it's a challenge to open my legs," Anahita replied, tilting forward, kissing her softly on the lips, which completely defused her annoyance.

"It'll be one if I cut your legs off," she answered, sticking her tongue out and dragging it up Anahita's nose.

"Gross Tara," Anahita muttered, wiping the spit off her nose, making her want to do it again.

She could hear Lanying chuckling and her annoyance quickly returned. Fixing Lanying with a 'what's so funny look', Lanying stopped laughing and presented her with what she considered to be a very fake, warm smile.

"As you already know from our first meeting, I'm not accustomed to being around people who are not my kind. Truth be told, after coming here I'm honestly happy for it. I find mingling a bit abrasive, yes abrasive is the first non-curse word that comes to mind.

If you're wondering why I'm laughing at your interactions, it's because you and a large majority of the people in your brigade, are the only people I've taken any true interest in since arriving here. Just from watching all of your small interactions, such as licking a person's nose, I can clearly see that all of you are close and value each other," Lanying said, sounding to Tara as if she'd rehearsed the warm words long before she'd meet any of them.

The problem was that Tara had felt her heart pounding in her chest the moment Lanying began to speak. As if her very words had the power to induce fear.

"Is she using her Mind-Bender powers on me? Messing with me? She's probably still not over me cursing her out about the metals after the briefing. She clammed up and got pissy when I started asking the tough questions," Tara thought, searching Lanying face for tells.

"If you're in my head right now bitch, you played off nothing. I know you know more. Tell me everything you know about the metals in my body or I'll beat it out of you. I need to know if people with pieces of these beings inside them pose an immediate Imperial liability. What's to stop these beings from already knowing what we're doing or thinking? The metals could be transmitting every damn classified thing I know about the armada forming up in the debris ring right now. So speak up bitch!"

After thinking that, she waited a few seconds, but Lanying didn't bat an eye. Nonetheless, Tara was still convinced her bodies' reaction had something to do with Lanying mental presences, invading her in some unperceivable way.

"Maybe a different approach to make you open up," she thought, wondering how to lead the conversation, even though she was certain Lanying would know the true intentions behind her every word.

"People like to talk about themselves more than anything else in the universe," she remembered one of her favorite priestess telling her a long time ago, giving her a good idea.

"Thank you Lanying, but truth be told, women of the Yin't and Yin'n system are similar to Niya in many ways in terms of interacting with others. When we're born, our lives are planned out almost to the letter. Take me, for example. I was born on the planet Yin'n, which never receives light from either the White dwarf or the newly ignited Brown dwarf.

As a daughter of a naturally habitable planet, who's bathed in perpetual darkness that shouldn't be possible yet occurs due to the odd workings of gravity and perfect timing, I was trained in what our Empire calls 'The one true path of the Divine Woman'. Women of Yin'n are chosen for this path because 'Yin' or 'darkness' represents women, or more accurately, the darkness inside a woman's womb where unborn life can rest undisturbed from the brilliant and often painful light of the universe."

"I'm aware of that, and I'm also well aware of your home systems odd solar systems' dynamics," Lanying said, appearing confused at the point she was trying to make.

"And I'm aware you want to deflect this conversation, but you don't know everything about my solar system's culture, because we normally keep what I'm about to tell you between ourselves," Tara thought, not missing a beat as she continued to speak.

"Yes I'm sure you are, but I find it necessary to describe everything so that you have a better sense of my solar systems' culture and how we relate to the Niya."

"Sure Tara, please continue."

"Thank you Lanying. So, because I was brought up following the one true path of the Divine Woman, I'm actually not supposed to be here. All of my warrior training focuses on the women of Yin'n only protecting their home system.

Anahita on the other hand was born on the planet Yin't, which is locked in a really strange tidal lock orbit with Yin'n. This tidal lock orbit, combined with our planets' irregular horseshoe orbit throughout our binary system makes it so that Yin't' is always bathed in the light of both our stars."

Tara smiled reassuringly to Lanying while checking her mood and could see she was still unwilling to take the bait.

"Just a little more, I know you're too damn prideful not to say 'we Niya' at some point," she thought as she said, "so what I'm getting at is that I understand how you feel when you relate to things in terms of your culture, as I'm always baffled that I am where I stand today. Anahita's planet Yin't represents a child's birth into the light of the universe, in which they're destined to venture out on their own. It also represent a kunuss opening during birth because it's said that for a split second as the child fully leaves the mother's womb, the interior is bathed in the same universal light.

So instead of me being out here, it's Anahita's path to venture out of our mother solar system, fighting wars in faraway places. And on this path, she seems to have also taken on the duty of trying to steal the man I'm fond of, with even more sinister plans of taking his virginity.

I cannot and will not let that happen. There's not a chance in the seven lives I'd miss the opportunity of being the first woman to make fun of every single one of his awkward moments, especially since he's already shown me he's scared of cumming too fast. Little does he know, I fully intend on making his fear a reality," Tara said as she purposely envisioned Banderas's face in the temple, enjoying the memory and hoping it could shield some of her inner thoughts if Lanying were truly prying around in her mind.

"I see... in my culture...we Niya..."

Tara held her breath, then did everything in her power to keep herself from shaking her head in shock that her plan had worked. She knew that even Lanying was surprised at herself, because she'd very noticeably balked right after the words had come out of her mouth. Not wanting Lanying to have a chance to recover, Tara nodded and quickly asked, "In your culture?"

She watched Lanying flush for a second before saying, "in my culture, we say Yin for the darkness in which life and existence manifest, symbolizing woman. And Yang for male, the light or he who walks in the universal light after he is born from the darkness. Together, we represent the pair in a flowing circle of black and white, with an entity of both darkness and light placed within each other, symbolizing their eternal union.

We'd thought it odd to hear a variation of Yin with the sound 'N' and 'T' added to the end. It seems your culture only focuses on the divinity of the woman and not the divinity of the union between man and woman. But if were speaking of literal darkness and not the creational kind, Anahita is right. The man you're fond of has something very dark inside of him. Well, I should say something darker than most. Truth be told, I've never born witness to a soul such as his. He has great potential to become a formidable warrior against the threat we all face."

Tara felt her heart pounding again, and this time she felt bile rising in her throat.

"Could one of you ladies get me some milk tea?" She asked, looking toward the five women who'd huddled up to talk amongst themselves, undoubtedly about the new additions to the squad.

"Sure thing," she heard Nana say as she turned her attention back to Lanying.

"You okay sweetie?" Lanying asked in a warm sweet voice, making Tara's lower back tighten.

"Yhea, I'm alright, I was wondering what you mean about Bandares. I mean I see potential, but the way you speak, well…it seem like you see something way more than potential."

"Yes Tara, I do mean more. In my culture we have a saying, but truth be told, the saying is nothing. I should say we have a practice we instill since birth."

Tara stared at Lanying waiting to hear the rest, all the while she could feel Anahita's uneasiness growing with each passing second.

"So it's not just me right?" She asked Anahita telepathically.

"The moment she came in, she gave me the creeps. And the first thing she did even as I bowed to greet her was ask about Bandares and Yon'tu. Honestly, I wish she was in the void with them. I umm… didn't even put her in the countdown. I don't know how she knew I was opening the airlock," Anahita replied in her mind.

"Your practice Lanying?" Tara said annoyed that Lanying hadn't finished what she was saying and was now looking back and forth between Anahita and herself as they spoke mind to mind.

"Oh yes. I'm sorry, I got a little side-tracked," Lanying replied, presenting another warm, reassuring smile.

"She probably knew because she's a Niya Mind-Bender. You heard of them right? Apparently they have similar abilities as our Mind-Stealers," she said to Anahita while smiling as brightly as she could, knowing Lanying knew her smile was just to bare her teeth.

"Ummm. So why are you still talking so openly if you're sure she can hear us?" Anahita replied in her mind, sounding nervous.

"Too see how much of a nosey bitch she is for one, and because I don't answer to this creep. The bitch can eat my mid-cycle discharge," she replied, nodding her head, still smiling as brightly as she could, making sure her eyes were locked with Lanying's.

"Yes, so my people believe in something called – 'Development of the Individual'," Lanying said, sounding unsure of her own words.

"Don't we all?" Tara blurted, too quickly for her own liking.

"See, this is why I say the phrase means nothing. Actions speak louder than words. If I may speak candidly?"

"I would never dream of stopping you, Lanying," Tara said, wishing she could cut the woman's tongue out.

"From my observations, your, I mean our Empress," Lanying corrected.

"If she is disrespectful to the Empress who saved her sorry ass people one more

time!" Tara thought, stepping back to give herself some much needed distance between Lanying and herself.

Lanying moved closer, and Tara almost lost her composure.

"From my observations after coming on board, I can see our Empress's idea was correct, yet lacking."

"Excuse?" Tara asked, channeling energy to her hand.

"At the end of the briefing the other day, I said I hope the pressure the Empress applied and the darkness embedded in everyone souls was enough to save us all.

"Yes I remember, that was the exact moment my dislike of you turned to hatred. Thank you for reminding me, I was having a hard time recalling that sudden shift. It's not even what you said, because I agree. I hope the darkness we hold within us can aid in the destruction of our enemy as well.

My problem with you is the way you said it. You sounded like you got off on the thought of billions suffering as they're forged into monsters. I'm even willing to bet one of my lives if I'd looked at your legs at the time, I'd have caught a glimpse of a quiver or two."

She studied Lanying's face, hoping to catch a guilty reaction; instead, Tara saw only mild shock.

"To be honest, I'm not a nice person, not at all. And I never plan on becoming one in the future. But I'm way too selfish to get my climax from the suffrage of others, that'd require me to think about people I don't care about," Lanying replied, nodding self-affirmably.

"I know a lot of 'not-nice' people and they don't creep me out like you," Tara said, balling her fist, taking another step back.

"Here's the thing about culture, about our Imperial culture. It's lacking what comes after the application of pressure. There's no set direction in which our Empress aimed the darkness inside people's souls. She went through all the trouble of creating environments and situations in which only the strong, manipulative, or highly adaptable could survive, and then what?

At every waking hour on this voidship, there's conflict. All I see are groups embedded in groups, all wanting to subjugate and dominate each other. Subjection, domination…which lead to many forms of unpleasant violations," Lanying said, looking her up and down, making Tara feel self-conscious about what had happened to her and her brigade a few days prior.

"So what are you getting at? My whole life I figured that's the point. Trap us all together, locked in hatred - a vicious cycle that make us darker and stronger with every cycle that passes. If we can't survive around each other's cruelty, how could the Empress rely on us to survive the cruelty of others? Especially at the hands of beings that are not human?" Tara stated, un-balling her fist, still keeping her full attention on Lanying's jaw.

Lanying started sniffing the air and Tara unconsciously began looking around for any potential threats.

"What do you sense? Is there danger? There are no explosives in this airlock," she said frankly, looking around to visually inspect the various items secured throughout the bay just to be certain, even though her implants had already told what was there.

"No, no danger or explosives. I just thought I caught a whiff of a woman's climax. Could that've been yours? Getting off on your grand speech about what your Empress wants?" Lanying said sarcastically, fixing her with an amused look.

I should be mad, but it's actually really funny how she swung that comment right back in my face. Anyways, how long does it take to get milk tea?" She thought, raising her hands in the air.

"I yield, your sharp wit has left me with nothing to say," Tara replied, tipping her head to Anahita, which was her way of saying Lanying impressed her.

"Development of an individual. And she discusses culture and our shortcomings when it comes to aiming darkness within ourselves. Okay, I see she may have a point."

"So Lanying, Development of the individual…meaning develop the person's darkness, to have a direction, so it's not wasted on ripping apart one's peers? Am I correct?"

"Exactly so. We teach our warriors to emulate a black hole, to concentrate all of the negativity surrounding them until it becomes a tiny, yet powerful focal point. The goal is to make sure they keep this black hole as concentrated as possible so that it doesn't consume others around it. Does that make sense?"

Tara visualised what Lanying was saying and understood the basic concept, but in her mind the concept had just as many flaws as the one she and her people were subjugated to.

"Makes sense, but what happens when the black hole eats its intended enemy? Black holes still continue to grow once they've consumed mass. Wouldn't said persons black hole grow to a point where it cares not who it consumes?"

"You impress me beyond comprehension for knowing what I was getting at when I brought up development of the individual, and from this question. It's a good thing humans are not black holes. Luckily, we have an ability to counteract any negativity that grows too strong, thus allowing us to wield a black hole's power, yet not be of their full nature.

This is honestly the real reason why I was laughing at your playful interactions earlier. So far, you and the ladies you have trained before coming here are the only ones that remind me of my people - concentrated darkness surrounded by love and light," Lanying said, walking closer as she spoke until she was almost face-to-face with her.

Tara didn't move away this time, wondering why Lanying took the time to tell her this.

"He'll need a lot of light to surround him as he becomes a black hole, and I fear only you may be able to supply it. And that scares me, because at any given moment in the war to come, you could die," Lanying whispered, presenting a small quadruple helix-shaped crystal in her right hand that awoke a suppressed memory of when the metals first entered her body as a child.

"I know this shape, this was what I saw when they finally stopped playing in the corners of my vision. This is the shape they made when they went into my feet as I stood at the water's edge. I must've only been five cycle old at the time. Lanying, you can see how concerned I am, yet you're really not going to give me a straight answer about the metals in my body are you?" She whispered, taking the crystal, which sent a vibration through her body and also caused her to feel slightly queasy.

Tara saw Lanying smiling with her mouth closed, and for a moment she saw a hint of mischief light up in her eyes.

"The new advancements I gave you the other day are very useful, but I feel they're becoming a bit generic as more people receive them. Especially since the many possibilities of alchemic manipulation are still finite. But this, I made just for you. Study its design and enhance it accordingly, then use your command powers to edit your people's weapons and armour further. You're very clever, and when you figure out what this is, I'm sure your enhancements will be something that'll make my base line creation look like child's play," Lanying whispered even lower than before as she leaned in towards her ear.

"And I think one day, I might take you up on the snack invite, if it's from the source of course."

With that, Lanying gracefully stepped away and walked out of the airlock, leaving Tara's mind racing as her body energy already began deciphering much of the coding inside the quadruple helix crystal.

Now the question is, why couldn't you just say the things encoded in this crystal to me in person. If you didn't feel safe just saying it, you could've easily put this in my mind, or used your implants to send over the files. Why do you trust this touch method? And who do you not trust which would make you feel this method was best? Is there a Mind-Stealer or Infiltrator on this ship you suspect is working against the Empire? And the thing I want to know most of all, is why in the seven lives do you trust me?" She thought, feeling the buzzing sensation increase as the information scribed itself into broken portions of her DNA.

"You okay?" Anahita asked, pushing her on the shoulder, snapping her out of a flashback of her childhood playing on the beach, jumping in puddles filled with grey and black liquid metals.

"Yhea, I'm okay. Anyways, how long have they been gone, and seriously how long does it take to get milk tea?" She asked, wrapping her armor around the crystal, while turning towards the airlock blast door just in time to see Nana rushing in with a bloody nose and a steaming mug.

"Hey, they're going out there, they're going out there!"

"What? Who is going where?" Tara asked, trying to figure out why Nana had a bloody nose and why she wasn't keeping it from dripping into the contents of the cup.

"The other brigades! They're going out into the void today! Today was supposed to be our day to space the rookies!" Nana screamed, sounding almost hysterical.

"So, who cares, even if most of them are from the debris clans, they're not experts in deep void. That's why I asked Sandreaka to take us away from the main debris trails, that way none of the rookies would have a big advantage. They'll all just be flailing around too scared to fight.

By the time they get their bearings, they'll all want to get back inside before they pick their stupid fights. So relax, rookies never like being deep in the void, actually I can't think of anyone who was comfortable on their first go into deep void, can you?" Tara asked, moving her finger to Nanas bloody nose to check if her implants had set it correctly.

"Oww Tara! Really now? Anyways! The other brigades are not sending their rookies out! They're sending out their voidship assault squads!" Nana exclaimed, sounding like she was two seconds away from slugging her.

"Oh damn it," Tara whispered, reaching for the blood-covered cup, taking a sip of the tea as she watched Anahita and the other woman form their helmets around their heads.

"Well... I wanted to see Bandares and this is what I get," she thought as

131

she formed her helmet.

Hearing a foot step, she turned and saw Yon'tu with one foot in the airlock and one foot out, holding a sandwich in one hand and a cup of something steaming in the other. Locking eyes with her through her helmet, he smirked, then stepped back out the airlock.

"Cocky, selfish asshole," she thought as the airlock opened before she could swallow the blood infused milk tea.

"I guess I'm lucky to get smart ones like him though. But to think he'd skip the brainwash ceremony and come sit casually in the medical bay! But maybe he did that out of fear. The metals were wrapped around his entire brain and small intestine by the time Lolina and I were able seal them. So there's no telling what he was going through. And he couldn't risk telling his old unit leaders he was suffering. Anybody halfway intelligent would know those two bitches were dumber than void rocks."

"Anahita, I just saw one of yours coming into the bay. Crazy huh?" She said, adjusting her visual settings to see clearly in the void.

"Yhea, I tracked him as he came back, which was almost right away. Something's up with him for certain."

"That's why I put him with you," Tara said playfully, even though she meant it.

"I don't see any of the other brigades out here, just our people. Are you sure Nana?" Anahita said over the coms.

"Yes, I am sure! I saw them mustering up in the airlocks on my way back from the mess!"

"And you got your bloody nose when?" Anahita asked mockingly, beating Tara to it.

"Before I got to the mess. My fist were itching really bad, so I had slug one or two people."

"Just one or two?" Tara replied, bursting into laughter, knowing Nana's vindictive nature all too well, having been the relief for those itchy fist for more reasons than she'd dare count.

"Or possibly four or umm, maybe a bit more... anyways, when I saw the other brigades mustering in the airlocks, I could see some of the squad leaders punching the manual override over and over. Looks like you made a good friend Tara," Nana said lightheartedly, making her smile.

"Oh! So you heard? News travels fast, huh? Let me ask her what's going on. She's been way to quiet come to think of it," she said, calling Sandreaka telepathically.

"I'm here Tara, I'm here! Sorry I've been so quite! I've been trying, but I can't stop them! I am arguing with all of the upper

Generals and my Admiral, all at the same time. Hold on okay?" Sandreaka replied.

"Okay," Tara responded, wondering what the outcome would've been if she hadn't become friends with Sandreaka.

"AH! You know what!? I'm coming out there to help retrieve your people! Screw this!" Sandreaka said angrily in her mind.

"No, no, it's okay," Tara replied, doing a head count of the people still in the void.

"Sixty five thousand newbies still out. And Anahita already sent out the call for everyone to come out and get their people. So we should be able to handle it," she thought, aiming herself towards two men who were tumbling relatively near to her location.

"No, I'm coming out there with ten thousand void spheres to help! If they want to play this game of 'it's just a drill', then I can play that too. I did all I can to block them, but the higher ups just threatened to sun toss me if I continue. Be alert, they're coming out now," Sandreaka said in her mind.

"This is karma for when I said - if we can't survive around each other's cruelty, how could the Empress rely on us to survive the cruelty of others - to Lanying earlier. She must've thought I was stupid for saying that, thinking if we kill ourselves how can we serve our Empress," Tara whispered to herself, latching onto the two men.

"It's okay, it's okay," she said reassuringly after opening a com channel to the two men, just in time to hear an earful of panicked cries for help.

"My position is not to mull over things I can do nothing about. If people want to fight my brigade, so be it," she thought mentally commanding the thrusters in her armor to fire, quickly steadying the men.

"Blue Star brigade! The other brigades are challenging us in the void! Get your asses out here, let's have some fun!" She screamed over the coms.

Thousands of voices cheered back through the coms making her smile as she watched the other brigades just starting to rise out of the airlocks.

"You idiots are sending out your best of the best. I just called out my entire brigade. Are you idiots still sure you want to run your so-called drills?" She bellowed over the coms after switching the channel to the 'All hands' setting.

In the first three minutes, they continued rising into the void, forming perfect five-man circle-formations, but one after the other, the five-person teams slowed down, realising they were becoming

CRJ Riggins

surrounded by rookies and their experienced squad members in front, and the rest of her brigade, which were all experienced behind them.

"Can't go back now! And I don't care who you are, you don't want to go forward, unless you want to come out as far as we are. We all know strange things happen deep in the void!" She shouted, knowing even the most experienced people knew better than to go too far, because strange things really did happen to people deep in void.

She also knew they'd realised if they were to charge her location or blow past her to reach her rookies and their squads, the people in her brigade behind them would move up to her location, cutting them off from returning to the ship entirely.

"That's what I thought!" She shouted, turning her head in the direction of Bandares's and T'mot's signal which to her disdain, were the farthest out compared to any in her brigade.

"Sandreaka, two of mine are three times the damn distance away from the rest!"

"I see them, I'm on my way. We don't want your love to get taken by the mysterious shadow void beings, do you...ooooohhhh!" She heard Sandreaka shriek playfully.

"Not funny! As a Void Assault, you of all people should know the Wayang are real! If they weren't, then why are the most experienced always so afraid to go too far?"

"Don't know, because void egress training for people like me who are natural in the understandings of the void can get their asses back into a voidship right after they're sucked out. I think people meant to follow the Void Assault path have a natural common sense ability to avoid unnecessary danger which prevents them from finding out if beings like the Wayang exist in the first place. This kind of common sense is what I think most Ground Assault people lack...correction ignore because they always have this unyielding need to be brave and fight something head on," Sandreaka said mockingly.

"Ha! That explains that slimy prick Yon'tu!"

"What?"

"Nothing...nothing...hey if what you're saying is true...then your dumb ass threats to me about assessing me for void competency is unnecessary. Even if I did better, I'm guilty as charged for ignoring common sense and running head first into danger! I'd never be able to maintain a voidship command, all the lovers of common sense under me would revolt!"

"Tara! Do you feel that?" Sandreaka screamed, sending chills up Tara's spine.

134

"Sandreaka?" She called out, worried when Sandreaka went silent for longer than thirty seconds.

"Don't you sense that?"

"No, I don't! What are you- Wait, yes I do! What is that?!" She stammered, turning her attention to the 'Voice of Kali' where she felt the ominous presence.

At first she saw nothing, but then she saw a shimmering lens-effect on the hull of the sphere.

"That's an entanglement point...on the hull of the ship? Everyone move away from the main voidship now!" Tara screamed, watching a large portion of the voidship molt and peel away as small golden orbs no bigger than cherries pummeled into the opening.

Wherever the golden orbs struck, Tara saw roots and tree limbs begin to grow.

"Oh no! We're still nowhere near ready for this," She whispered in horror.

Chapter XI

I like your theory, it suits me

BANDARES BROUGHT HIS ELBOW DOWN on T'mot's armored face, sending T'mot's entire body spinning around. He'd almost went careening off as well, but having gotten used to the armor controls, he quickly brought himself back in line with T'mot again.

"Why couldn't you just leave me alone, huh?" Bandares grunted, timing T'mot's spin perfectly before sending out a violent kick to his head, sending T'mot hurtling deeper into the void.

"You know, I knew you were going to come after me when we got out here?" Bandares snarled, catching up to T'mot.

"What? I can't hear you? Are you throwing up in there? I don't get why you're sick! Are you or are you not from one of the debris clans? Out in the void, you should be just fine! Don't you people debris hop using only armour suits? You and your groupies were always bragging about having your suit implants put in before us planet dwellers, so why in the seven lives are you throwing up? Aren't you used to being out here like this?" Bandares asked, becoming even more aggravated at the fact that T'mot wasn't answering his questions.

All of a sudden, an odd feeling went through his body that almost drove him mad with fear. Then, just at the edge of his vision, he saw something darker than blackness of the void moving over his and T'mot's body. Less than a second later, T'mot started screaming at the top of his lungs.

"Oh shut up!" Bandares growled, shaking his head, trying to clear away the blackness surrounding his vision.

"Looks like tentacles of a river octopus," he thought, feeling chills run up his spine as the smoke-like tentacles continued wrapping around

them.

"Help me! Ahhh help me! Please! Please! It hurts! It hurts so bad!" T'mot screamed through the coms.

Banderas felt the searing pain as well, first in his hands, then traveling throughout the rest of his body, but unlike T'mot, he refused to scream. Watching T'mot withering in agony just a few feet away actually started to make him happy, and as the pain increased and T'mot's wailing grew louder, Bandares found himself laughing hysterically.

"Ten cycles of your big mouth and selfishness! Ten cycles of passive aggressive crap, always playing tough, and now you're wailing like a baby!" Bandares thought with disgust.

Taking a deep breath, he focused all of his anger and hatred on T'mot, and somehow the pain quickly began to subside.

"I have the perfect idea!" He thought, recalling their fight in the barrack's chamber.

"T'mot! I'll help you! I am almost there! I am almost there!" He said dramatically.

"Pa...pa...pa...pleaseee!!!! It hurts so! Ahhhh!" T'mot screamed, almost unable to even speak through the agony.

"I'm coming! T'mot! I'll save you!" He said, trying to hold in his laughter, but eventually failing.

"Ha! I bet you believed me for a moment! That I'd actually come help you! Don't you remember your lessons for me? Never trust your enemy, and lying to deceive the enemy is of the utmost honor?! Or have you forgotten your lessons so quickly?!" He asked T'mot, through spouts of laughter.

"I'm...Sorry! Please help me," T'mot whimpered weakly, causing Bandares's laughter to become pure hysterical mirth to the point where he actually felt his kudock had become fully erect.

He no longer even felt the pain from the smoke-like tentacles wrapped around his body. Looking down in curiosity, he could see the tentacles peeling off of him till all that remained were two, wrapped tightly around his balled fist.

"Ummm no! I don't think I will T'mot! Remember what you said!? It's every man for himself!"

"NO!!!" T'mot screamed.

"Yes T'mot, I like your theory, it suits me!" Bandares said, honing in on where he wanted to strike.

"Hey T'mot! Guess what?"

"Nooo pleassssss!!!"

"You'll be one less man for any of us to worry about!" Bandares screamed, lunging forward, punching T'mot as hard as he could on the armor located over his right kidney, sending him careening off with the tentacles.

Before he could even blink, T'mot vanished along with the tentacles around his hands and the darkness surrounding his vision completely receded, leaving him feeling more alive than he'd ever felt in his entire life. Letting lose a victorious primitive howl, he finally realised Tara had been speaking to everyone in the brigade through the coms the entire time he'd been fighting T'mot, both from the tone in her voice, and from the fact that he was hearing her words in the middle of her sentence.

"Oh crap! What'd she say?" He thought frantically, turning his body around just in time to see a large chunk of the main voidship shear clean off, while tiny golden orbs slammed into the exposer, which he imagined were crystal beads firing from some type of kinetic projectile weapon.

Suddenly, he felt gravity take hold of him. Falling backward onto his rear, he looked up to find himself in an airlock that could only fit about twenty people.

"Hey, get your ass up here now!" He heard a slightly familiar female voice say over the ship's PA.

Hopping up, he turned and followed instructions uploaded to his implants, which led him through a set of blast doors, then up a steep ramp leading to the bridge of the voidship. When the blast door to the bridge opened up, he could see curved rows of empty concaves in the deck.

"Hop in one, rookie!" The woman said in a harsh tone of voice.

Before he could even take a step, the voidship rattled, then listed heavily to port, sending him tumbling into the fourth concave from the blast door. The moment he fell in, a translucent crystal semi-sphere sprang up and enclosed him in. Standing up in the concave, he saw a layer of red-yellow metals that reminded him of his trident covering the translucent crystal to the point where he could no longer see anything on the bridge.

"This will hurt a bit," he heard the woman's voice say from inside the encasement as wires sprung out from every direction, lodging themselves into his body armour.

He barely felt a thing. All he cared about was figuring out what was going on outside.

"Voidship crew is easy and hard, all in one. Easy, because almost everything you think, the ship will try to facilitate within reasonable means. Call up the view outside," the woman ordered him.

Bandares did as she asked and immediately felt overwhelmed, not only could he see three hundred sixty degrees in every direction at once, but he could also see in spectrums he'd never thought possible.

"Here's the hard part: too much information. And, you can't just filter everything away. Everything you're being shown, you need to know how to use, all at the same time, or else you'd might as well be shooting and flying blind."

"She should've just said it's hard. I haven't even had time to open her profile icon and it's been flashing since she scooped me out of the void. How in the seven lives does she expect me to get used to all this information?" he wondered, opening her profile.

"Admiral Sandreaka?" He whispered in surprise, recalling why he'd recognised her voice.

"What?"

"Nothing, just..." he began, then opted not to ask.

"What am I doing out here, rescuing you while you were in your blind stupid rage? Didn't you hear your girlfriend call your brigade to arms? I take your silence as a no. And I saw what happened to the guy you were wailing on. I'd say you're lucky, but I'm honestly too freaked out you survived against such a thing... and from what you did to him."

"He deserved it. I hope whatever it was traps him in pain and agony for the remainder of his six lives," Bandares mumbled, looking down to see why he felt a warm sensation running over his body armor.

"I can see why she likes you. Anyways, pay attention. Auto fire only does so much, fighting in the void always needs a living being's touch. So, that means I need you to assess the situation while you're aiming, then fire. Some targets are going to be obvious; others, you need to use your gut feeling. Now make yourself useful while I scoop up your girlfriend and a group of others," Sandreaka said as hundreds of red and violet target icons formed in his mind.

"This is too much to take in! And girlfriend? Who, Tara? Or Anahita? I hope she's talking about Tara!" He thought, seeing a stream of golden orbs heading their way.

Less than a second later, he felt a vibration and then nothing. In his mind, a short video played out, showing him that the sphere he was standing inside of had detached from the main body of the voidship and was now being held in place magnetically in order to buffer him as the ship took hits.

"What's the liquid?" He asked the ship.

It immediately responded with another video showing him that it was a multipurpose gel for sealing hull breaches and body armor as well as for healing wounds on a person's body.

"Target priority?" Flashed in his mind as orange and yellow target icons sprung up in every direction, showing areas the red and violet icons hadn't already annotated.

Some of the orange target icons even zoomed in close enough to where he could make out what he thought looked like swamp tress growing out the sides of the main voidship.

"Ummm! Ummmm!!! Hey! Umm!!" He said aloud.

"She's on board now, don't worry."

"Huh?"

"Your girlfriend."

"My who? Umm! Trees are in the void! Trees are in the void! Is that normal to have tress in the void? Or is there something wrong with the sensors?" He shrieked, hoping the sensors were broken.

"I'll remember you didn't know who Sandreaka was referring to," he heard Tara say.

"Tara! I mean General!" He exclaimed thanking the Goddesses' Kali and Vajrayogini at the same time for allowing him to hear her voice again.

"Nope, don't want to hear it Bandares. Sandreaka, I think priority fire should be the entanglement point. What do you think?"

On the right side of his mind's eye view, small icons appeared showing Sandreaka, Tara, and what looked like his entire squad minus T'mot and Yon'tu, plus the addition of seven other people he didn't know, but could see by the 'Blue Star' text above their names, they were part of his brigade.

"Sounds good, but we've got to make sure to fluctuate metals and crystal consistently or the spores will adapt even before they sprout into trees," Sandreaka responded.

"I am out of my league," he whispered to himself, watching streams of energy and projectiles hurtling towards locations just in front of the 'Voice of Kali', intercepting some of the golden orbs of light before they smashed into it.

"The rest of you fire at anything that doesn't look human," Sandreaka commanded.

Immediately after, Bandares saw more energy beams and kinetic projectiles spew out, smashing into hundreds of branches and vines growing throughout the main voidship.

"Okay then," he said to himself, willing the ship to fire a mix of kinetic explosive projectiles as well as energy beams in the same location as everyone else.

Watching his fire connect with the branches and vines, he felt a strange calming satisfaction, which made him redouble his efforts.

"I can get used to this. This view is of heat sources. This one is light wave lengths. This is radio transmissions. And this one is atom entanglement and oscillations. Okay! I'll layer the images like this," he thought excitedly, stacking the images in such a way that everything had relevance and continuity to the other.

"I need more information to predict when and where the branches will fire, so I'll place the image of electromagnetic waves here, and gravity waves here. Oh! And particle distribution here. I also need to avoid shooting people! Damn there's a lot out there, so I should say avoid shooting too many people. So I'll put the human electromagnetic fields here, and human brainwaves here. Now layer it! Perfect! Wow! There's a lot more people out there I hadn't seen before! Sorry to anyone I've already sent to the next life! Oh crap! That branch looks like it's about to fire! I'll take it out first!"

"Yes, I can do this!" He exclaimed in a hushed voice as the branch he targeted ripped to shreds.

His excitement was short lived as branches and vines nearest to his target that had only been marred by his fire began to grow back twice as thick.

"Hey! Some of them are breaking apart and some of them are growing! And anyone know what those yellow things are, coming out the branches that are breaking apart?" Bandares asked pensively, unsure what to make of the new threat.

"The wavelengths' imagery lets you know how the beings are trying to adjust their bodies as well as which limbs are dying. Dying limbs reflect light differently. As for the way the enemy is adapting, some are mainly trying to protect themselves from crystals, and others, from metals. The only way to kill them is by using many types of metal, crystal, and energy in different alchemic combinations," Sandreaka instructed him.

As she spoke, Bandares saw a list of thousands of complex sacred geometrics scrolling across his vision.

"You see the geometrics? Each geometric is an alchemic formula in which you can choose to load the kinetic projectiles or the energy beams with. When you improve your alchemy skills, you'll be able to create your own alchemic formulas and add them to the list," Sandreaka said in a tutoring tone, giving him the feeling she enjoyed instructing him.

"I see, but how do I know which formula to use?" He asked, picking them at random, now firing his shots off with pristine accuracy, but growing increasingly frustrated that some of the limbs were benefiting from his efforts to kill them.

"Don't get discouraged! Some of the formulas you'll use have immediate effects, while others maim so someone else can make the kill. If you see it grow, use the different layers of imagery to study the properties that've changed, then pick a formula that works against it. Stop picking them at random, instead, try to read and understand the geometrics," Sandreaka said in a motherly tone, which failed to ease his anxiety.

"Listen up newbies! The larger these things grow, the faster they adapt. And the faster they adapt, the faster those beetle like beings that are just starting to appear, swarm out. Bandares, good scan layering, you were the first newbie who caught sight of the yellow beings. If you newbies injure a branch or vine, expect the yellow ones to come out. During my brief I was told to think of them kind of like white blood cells.

So I've been adding alchemic mixtures of powdered crystal and metal to my fire, hoping to poison their bodies if the kill shot doesn't work. And don't be fooled by those slow moving yellow blobs, I promise you, the way they're behaving is all a façade. In a moment's notice, they're going to be moving very fast, catching all sorts of people off guard. When they get to a person, they liquefy and take the person's body over. After that, they know everything that person knows, as well as being able to tap into their coms and pretend they're our peers," Tara instructed over the ships coms.

"I'd rather kill myself," Bandares whispered.

"You'd all better kill yourselves," Tara retorted.

"Enough with the killing ourselves talk, focus on killing them," he heard Nana mumble.

"Sandreaka, when you fought them before, how long did it take before they grew strong enough for the beetle-like beings to come out? A lot of them are starting to pour out of limbs that don't appear to be all that strong. Yhea, some of them are even starting to come out of the dying limbs. I want to say that doesn't make sense, but I don't really know. Is there anything we should be looking for, that wasn't covered in my brief with that creep Lanying?" he heard Tara ask.

"Lanying came to my chamber a few hours after she met with you and gave me the same mind-to-mind brief. Seems like she covered way more things than I knew, and honestly when we talked, it seemed like she was more interested in you Tara," Sandreaka replied, sounding somewhat somber to Bandares.

"Ahh! Of course she was! What a cruel sick joke the universe plays on me. I briefed my Generals and my squad leaders yesterday, and today, I wanted the rest of my brigade to be brought up to speed, but it seems they're fated to be terrorised directly from the source. And, this is no time to stop firing Bandares!" Tara screamed, causing him to jump.

The problem for Bandares was that he'd just watched a group of people floating in the void engulfed in yellow.

"So we'll have to kill our own once they're taken over right? Unless, maybe we can just cut them from our com networks for now, then collect them and purge the beings out later on?" He asked, still unable to swallow.

After twenty long seconds of no response, he opened fire on the people he'd seen taken over, feeling a sense of shame come over him after every shot.

"Sandreaka, are all our channels already compromised?" He heard Tara ask in a low-spirited tone.

"It doesn't matter, it's not just my command void sphere being attacked. The entire armada has just been hit. If it weren't for your request to have us move away from the main fleet gathering in the debris trail, we'd most likely all be dead," Sandreaka whispered.

Bandares hadn't even known he was a part of an armada, he'd thought he was aboard the only ship heading to the Adrasteian moon-worlds. Hearing the news was one thing, but when he mentally inquired about the status of the armada, images appeared in his minds of thousands of ships ripped apart by trees and vines. If the sight was not bad enough, all around, he could see dark red beetle-like beings swarming through the passageways of ships. As they moved, they fired energy beams from multiple appendages extending from their body, which completely emulsified people, body armor and all."

What an awful way to go to the next life. Wait, never mind," he thought, seeing people with skin and armor the same color as bright yellow pollen, moving throughout the ships using Imperial weapons to kill any who hadn't been taken over yet.

Bandares had thought the people taken over would move slow or disjointedly, but after just a few short moments of watching the video feed, he could see they were swift, accurate, and completely coordinated as they moved throughout the ships. He could also see from their twisted faces, with tears of bright red blood running down their cheeks that somehow they were still alive, forced to suffer through excruciating pain in which their only relief would come from death bestowed by former peer.

"I need to become stronger. I hope I survive this. I need to become so much stronger," he thought, closing the feed.

"We've been boarded!" Sandreaka screamed as the ship's alarm went off.

"Sandreaka, any tips on face to face? You're the only one who has dealt with them?" he heard Tara say over the alarm chime.

"Yhea, don't die!" Sandreaka replied.

"Not helping!"

"What'd Lanying tell you about face to face in the brief, Tara?"

"She said the new weapons are very effective! That'd be all well and good except I just got them a few hours after the brief and since most of my rookies were still in surgery, I had them upgraded first. I'm not having my rookies face these damned things without them learning how to fight in their respective squads, new weapons or not!

Seven lives, with my luck they'd end up impaling or shooting each other by accident! Oh! And just a little while ago, she gave me something else that might be able to help, if I had maybe a week or two to do something with it!" Tara proclaimed, leaving Bandares feeling helpless.

"Where are the invaders?" He asked the ship telepathically, wanting to know what they were up against.

The ship found them after a few seconds and zoomed in on them. Seeing the bright yellow bloated beings pressing up against a set of blast doors made his stomach turn, but as the fear of them taking over his body grew, an idea lit up in his mind.

"This fear is nothing compared to the fear I faced and conquered out in the void! This fear is absolutely nothing!"

"I'll go fight them!" He bellowed without thinking a second thought.

In response, there was a long silence and then he heard soft chuckles from almost every woman coming over the coms.

"I already fired every damn internal weapon on-board, and spaced half the chambers in the damn ship to get rid of them hero. Where were you six seconds ago?" Sandreaka asked sarcastically.

"Oh, I thought, I thought!"

"He was amping himself up Sandreaka, be nice. And Bandares, there's no way I was going out there to face them in my current state. I was just trying to sound brave because I knew she was going to do that. Also, didn't you just hear me you little ass? I said I'm not sending my rookies out to fight them. Even though I'm proud of you...I can tell you really meant your words," Tara said in a tone he found difficult to classify as either praise or condescending.

"Ah Tara, you tell me to be nice and then - oh no...my command ship...there's no way of saving it now. Damn these beings, they're the curse of my life. Fine then, I'll be theirs as well! I pray to the Goddess Kali to give me the strength and to the Goddess Vajrayogini to give me true clarity to carry out my conviction! As of this moment! I promise to dedicate all seven of my lives to eradicating these beings from each of the seven plains of existence!" Sandreaka blared over the coms, drawing Bandares's attention away from target images annotating the spaced compartments which he'd been firing profusely upon since discovering their location.

"At first I was worried. But now that I think about everything that just happened, why do I feel so good?" He reflected, watching thick-rooted branches burst out the main voidship in every direction engulfing and absorbing everything faster and faster with each passing second.

Seeing the last of the ship consumed, he pictured the men and woman he had seen waiting in front of his stasis pod becoming engulfed by branches, screaming in agony and thought, *"oh yes...this is the feeling of vengeance. I'm starting to really enjoy this feeling."*

Content with that thought, he fired with reckless abandon, no longer aiming at any one point in particular. Shortly after, he could see his mood had carried over as everyone else began to do the same.

"Wooow!" He shouted, feeling exhilarated.

"I'll help you fulfill your promise Admiral Sandreaka! If not in this life, then in all the others!" He bellowed over the coms as he watched the monstrosity of branch and vine continue to grow under their desperate fire.

'Hey! I love you Tara!" he said telepathically, as he screamed what he thought were obscenities at the enemy, knowing in his heart of hearts he wasn't going to have another opportunity to say how he felt, watching as the branches extended outwards towards them at speeds the voidship was unable to calculate.

Grinning ear to ear, he made a deal with the darkness inside himself, promising to always feed it in his remaining six lives. Telling himself he'd be a conqueror not a peon, a consumer not a giver, and the greatest promise he made to himself - was that he'd never be below anyone or anything, ever again.

"I...loov...like you to, you idiotic pain in the ass. You do know you declared it aloud, and in my head right? And now for the remainder of my lives, I'll never hear the end of it. You've even managed to beat the enemy Bandares. You've got every bitch in this voidship laughing so hard they're already halfway to next life from asphyxiation," Tara's warm sultry voice whispered over the coms as the branches and vine stopped just shy of their ship, wilting into thick grey sooty clumps that stretched out in every direction for miles.

Quivering head to toe from adrenaline coursing through his body, he scanned the void repeatedly and found that both the beetle-like beings and the bulbous yellow-beings had suffered the same fate. Knowing he knew only the bare minimum when it came to void warfare, he waited a full minute to see if anyone would speak up and explain what had happened. When no one spoke even a single word, Bandares started to get the feeling that the only true power the universe accepted and respected was the power of personal vengeance, thinking *"what other reason could the Goddesses have to keep me on this plain of existence, if not to take vengeance for myself and the people I care about?"*

Chapter XII

The only piece left

Two weeks after Takumbo received Lord General Bandares's memories

Imperial Date: 2141 ABCAE
Month, day: Phaophi, 1st

Location: The four moon sector, in the Globular Cluster of Tyche, aboard
World-Ship of 'Dimitrius's Ascension'

World-Ship population: Approx. One billion.

It's been three days since Emperor Dimitrius has been appointed as the new leader of Adrasteia
by former Emperor and Empress, Quortez and Felicia. Chaos has swept across the Empire with
billions rebuking their decision, with many stating that Emperor Dimitrius is simply not strong
enough to lead. Thousands who feel they're better suited for the role, including many of the
Empires most powerful Overseers, have invoked a rarely used Imperial rule, forcing Emperor
Dimitrius to fight a life or death match against any and all who wish to claim the throne within
the period of one Imperial week, which comprises of ten days.

One such person is Tier twenty-nine, Lord Admiral Nairn, which just so happens to be Lord
General Bandares's son.

TAKUMBO'S STOMACH WAS IN KNOTS transiting the entanglement
point from Adrasteia binary to the four moon sector. Immediately
upon her arrival, she found that the point had been moved
approximately forty minutes away from 'Dimitrius's Ascension', and
that was only if her void sphere traveled its maximum, which was
eighty percent the speed of light.

"Annoying," she muttered, biting her bottom lip, willing the
fluidic nano-material encompassing her to widen, giving herself space
to pace around.

As the matte black nano-material peeled away, a soft yet
distinctive chime went off, indicating that a Wayang vessel was
detected.

"Probably curious why I'm with child, yet alone in the void. It'll be funny if I

get scolded by a predatory race for being irresponsible," she thought as an image appeared, displaying the fetus in her body, next to an image of a floating question mark glyph.

"Yup they're scolding me, but I guess it could be worse. If my people find me out here, they'll be so pissed the Emperor himself would end up having to move the whole damn World-Ship to me," she mumbled, closing the picture without sending a response, mostly because she had no idea how to interact with beings who rarely ever interacted with humans unless it was to snatch them out of the void.

Another soft yet distinctive chime went off again, followed by an image that floated directly in front of her face displaying three smoke like ships in relation to her own.

"A flank formation? Now I'm being escorted by predators. Okay...I can get used to being with child," she said, chuckling to herself, yet wishing she could find more joy in her situation.

"I think I had Bandares's intentions all wrong. I don't think he's trying to punish himself at all," she mused, bringing up an image of Bandares, Tara, and Nairn in front of her, smiling at Nairn's features.

"You have your mom's nose, dad's big forehead, with that same scowl he makes. And you're selfish to challenge the new Emperor," she mumbled, rubbing her face in annoyance at the entire situation, blaming the new Emperor for most of the problem, having a gut feeling of what kind of man he truly was.

Calling up a live image of the arena positioned in the middle of the World-Ship, her stomach instantly turned at the amount of gore that was present. Like all ships in the Empire, the World-Ship was composed completely out of nano-material, which she was certain should've been able to handle the body parts. Then she realised that it wasn't struggling at all, and that the Emperor had changed the schedule of one of his fights in which he'd just called out a group of six thousand.

During the few moments she'd not been directly paying attention to the events taking place on the World-Ship, having been distracted by the Wayang's arrival, he'd killed them all. Now she could see the Emperor casually striding through the midst of the carnage, all while sipping a cup of coffee from a small nano-material mug.

"Killing people in the arena doesn't make people suddenly respect you as a leader. They were already too blind to see what your lazy demeanor truly meant, so now they're just going to make more excuses to challenge you. I guess, I can't really judge you. The things you must know, the things you must've experienced. I apologise for doubting your actions my Emperor. I just don't want Bandares

jumping in, trying to save his son, who in my opinion is already lost. Both of them may think they can win, but my gut knows for certain, no one can win against you," she thought as she restlessly placed her platinum ankh medallion into her mouth.

All of a sudden images of void spheres sprang to life in front of her, causing her to panic and spit the medallion out.

"Set course away?" Her ship asked in her mind, confused as to why she was panicking over the sight of friendly vessels.

"No, change cloak settings. Have we been detected?" She replied, already visualizing the stern lectures she'd receive and also afraid they'd hall her as far away from the World-Ship as possible, deeming it too dangerous for a woman with child.

"Energy collecting in forward sections of Wayang vessels, probable target are the void spheres just detected."

"Oh! Damn it!" She screamed, knowing there's nothing she could've done to stop the Wayang as they fired at the void spheres, simply vanishing afterwards.

"Really? Did you really just tell on me?" She snarled to no one in particular, seeing the odd, dark-violet burst of energy careening off the primary shields of the void spheres.

"How's the cloak configuration?" She asked the ship desperately.

"Tier one, Ground Assault Elite Takumbo, scans tells me you're with child! What are you doing traveling alone in the void?" She heard a man scream through her ship's nano-material.

"Damn it, need more time!"

Six, five million crew, oily-black void spheres sprung up all around her, with one moving directly in front of her own.

'Damn it! I won't get to speak to him in person. I'm done," she whispered as her void sphere seamlessly merged with the larger one.

Within seconds she was surrounded by twelve stern-faced men and women.

"Look, I can explain," she began.

"You were trying to fix your cloak settings to slip past us. Why?"

"Well, why were you cloaked?" She blurted, defensively just as her eyes took in the sight of two command chains in the form of trident medallions, which made her look down in shame for addressing the voidship's Admiral and one of his lower Admirals with disrespect.

"None of your business, seriously though, why alone? Call for escorts. Everyone would understand why you'd want to see Lord

General Bandares. But no, you tried to sneak! Do you know what it's like to get a nasty message from beings who eat us, pretty much asking humans why in the seven lives did we allow one of our life bringers to casually float around alone in the void?"

"I apologise Admiral. I assumed I'd get turned away. If it makes anyone feel any better, I was directly reprimanded by the Wayang as well. And then they, sort of, kind of, kept me safe by escorting me," she pleaded looking up, only to find everyone's face still locked in annoyance.

"You assumed? Would you like me to recite all the similes and metaphors that address the many flaws of assumptions?" The Admiral asked her, and from the tone of his voice, she could tell her reprimand was coming to a close.

"No Admiral, I am aware of them."

"Good, hands up, we want to lay our wishes, and then I'm sending you off with this squad through an intra-ship point. And do not speak to anyone of our presences or of the intra-ship points. Is this clear?"

Takumbo lifted her arms, nodding as people laid their hands on her stomach, leaving warm, loving sensations as they wished her and her child well. The last two people to give their wishes were the Admirals, who laid their hands while they knelt and kissed her stomach. Standing up, they made eye contact with her and the emotions that emanated off of them made her short of breath.

"They're in kill mode, and I bring an unborn child into their face, I'm really messing up their mindset. Why does my plan have to inadvertently involve others?" She wondered regretfully, breaking eye contact with them to stare fixedly at the designs of their ankh and trident necklaces.

Sensing their eyes seeking hers, but feeling too ashamed to re-engage, she looked away from their sacred jewelry, moving her eyes further down their bodies towards their waist chains which held their unformed weapons. Staring at the semi-translucent liquid orbs hanging lazily on the chains, she mused at how something that looks so simple could be so deadly. As she thought this, she unconsciously moved her hand towards her own unformed weapon hanging on her waist chain, truly understanding the conflict of emotion she was putting them through.

"Excuse me, I really didn't think my actions through. I thought it was going to be a fast trip, and I figured if there were any problems, I could take care of it. But I didn't think of how anyone would feel had I died with child. I also apparently didn't think of how higher Tier beings felt about eating lower Tier beings that are with child," she said, softly squeezing her unformed weapon, taking comfort in the warmth and vibration it resonated.

Takumbo heard soft scoffs coming from people after her last comment, but still didn't feel brave enough to look up.

"Admiral, my Tier ones are nervous, I can feel them from here. Takumbo, best wishes to you and your child," the lesser Admiral said, causing Takumbo to finally look up just in time to see her slide through the nano-material floor.

"All of my lesser Admirals, except her are nervous. Best wishes to you and your unborn child. And I hope if we ever encounter each other again, it's not via the introduction of a vicious race of sentient beings," the voidship Admiral said, who her internal nano-material only indicating as a Tier seven with no name or any form of personal bio afterwards.

"Something really dangerous is going down, he has only Tier level annotated, and the lesser Admiral had nothing displayed, not even a sarcastic alias name," she thought, feeling her heart beginning to pound as she realised the implications.

Nodding, she took a step back towards the squad of people that'd come behind her. When he returned the nod, the floor became liquid engulfing her along with her escorts. Within seconds they emerged inside an enormous chamber filled with warm, blue-green light.

"An invasion force," she whispered, watching as millions of people emerged out of various intra-ship points throughout the chamber to converge on one enormous intra-ship point positioned directly in the center of the chamber.

"Mind your business, leave dying to us, and life bring to yourself," a woman said, placing her hand on her lower back, escorting her to an intra-ship point that could probably only fit two people standing side by side at a time."

"This is one of Emperor Dimitrius's new alchemically advanced nano-ships, made to brainwash those captured from the Sai'nct and Cen'tia systems," Takumbo said rhetorically, feeling nano-material from the ship starting to flow into every portion of her body.

"Yes, this is a 'Versus ship'. Now get off of it," the woman said in a warm tone.

"Hold on, the ship is updating me," Takumbo said smiling and shaking her head, as she laid her hand on the woman's arm.

"No matter how integrated nano-material makes us, we still like to hear what's going on from the person's mouth. I guess small things like that remind us

that we're still human. It was also her way of saying to me that she didn't expect the 'Versus Ship' to update me. That tells me it'd be out character for any of the Admirals aboard this ship to grant me such clearance. So if not them, then who?" She wondered, feeling the update from the 'Versus ship' coming to a close.

When Takumbo felt the update complete, the woman smiled at her knowingly, then kneeled and kissed her stomach. Afterwards, the rest of the squad did the same.

"Hey, why are you bestowing even more blessing? Are all of you going to do this on the," the woman softly pushed her through the intra-ship point before she could finish.

"Oh damn it, I thought the first group was bad!"

"I see, so what he meant by escort is that my escorts will bring me to an intra-ship point, then call more escorts, who will be waiting for me here," she said sarcastically, staring at eleven stern-faced men and women whose ankh medallions were literally aglow with dark colors of aggravated emotional energy.

"They had things they were doing before you became an inconvenience, so we volunteered when they told us they were on their way with you. And unlike the majority of them, we do not find your actions amusing at all. Yet I dare say, we all agree your actions are regretfully understandable," a man said, shaking his head in annoyance.

The floor became liquid, engulfing all of them before she had a chance to open her mouth. A few moments later she found herself at the arena's edge, directly next to the Emperor's waiting area. To her delight, the first thing she saw was Bandares staring at her with a look between welcome and scorn that made her want to burst out laughing.

"You! Ah! There are no words that can describe my frustration towards you!" She shouted, wanting to knock the scowl off of his face.

As she spoke, the men and women of the squad had moved closer, forming a tight semi-circle in which she only had a clear line of sight with Bandares.

"It's not safe here. Anyone on this side of the arena is a sympathiser of Emperor Dimitrius and there've already been several attacks carried out on both the waiting area and the seats closest to it," Bandares said to her as he scanned the general area.

"I know," she replied, glancing between her escorts to take a look at the Emperor and his lover, whom many like herself were already calling Empress.

When her eyes had rested upon the woman, the woman immediately felt it and turned towards her. Smiling brightly, she flapped her hand up and down, inviting her to step fully into the waiting area. Bowing her thanks, Takumbo walked through the shields into the oval-shaped waiting area with her guards surrounding her every step of the way.

Coming up to Bandares, who stood almost a solid foot shorter than her even six feet, she looked down into his eyes and took hold of his arms. Bringing them up, she studied his hands made of nano-material, taking in the details of the claws he'd chosen to use as fingers.

"This is where the Wayang had grabbed your hands. Is this why you have no hands? Did they infect you with something where you had to cut them off?" She asked in a hushed tone.

"Where'd you leave off in my memories? I take it you haven't seen much of the things I've done, or else you wouldn't be here," he said nodding his head in self affirmation before breaking eye contact with her to gaze across the arena.

Following his line of sight, she could see Nairn standing in the opposition's waiting area with his legs parted, arms folded behind his back, and a sickly blue aura surrounding his body.

"Almost the same color aura as your father's. It's odd how a few hues difference can change a color from beautiful to sickly," she thought as she said "for weeks on end, I watched you having nightmares about your son's fate, and all the while, I've been having nightmares about yours. Then today, I finally realised you're planning to fight the Emperor before your son has a chance to. And I know you might think I'm selfish and shouldn't have a say in the matter, but I really don't want you to."

"What else do you expect me to do? He's the last piece of her I have left. He's the only way I can still see her face, the only way I can say I'm sorry for what I've done to her," Bandares said softly as tears welled up in his eyes.

Hearing his words and seeing the tears that had welled up in his eyes beginning to run down his cheeks, she desperately wanted to say something to make him feel better.

"Listen, there's got to be a way to talk Nairn out of this. His fight is in four days, so we have time. Please, I'm begging you, don't rush into the arena with the Emperor until we come up with a better solution," she choked out, knowing her words were empty, recognizing that any person willing to display an aura of pure malice wouldn't be able to be swayed by words.

"She'll never forgive me in any of our remaining lives if I don't even make an attempt to save our son's life," Bandares sputtered out through his sobs, turning to look at her, almost as if he were begging her to say Tara would forgive him.

"She will forgive…" she started to say, stopping when Bandares shook his head, no.

"Even if I manage to save him, I doubt she'd forgive me in any of the remaining lives. You'd know why, but you must've not gotten that far yet. Where've you stopped? Have you seen, what I've done to Wa'raydon or the rest of the people of Ah Tabai?

What you learned about the war on Ah Tabai is a crock. The things I've done were so awful even the historians couldn't stomach it. So they only focused on the battles, not what I did in the lulls between them, which is honestly where most outcomes of battles and wars are decided."

"I can't believe you lived to speak about something you did to Lord Admiral Wa'raydon. He's the true meaning of evil, even more so than Nairn. In training, the Overseers would show us images of him in one void battle after another. As if he thirsted for things to constantly die under his fire. I couldn't even look at those cold black eyes for a full second without feeling like they were consuming my soul," she reflected, feeling the small of her back reflexively tighten in fear, just from the memory of his cold pale muscular face, and matte black nano-material eyes.

Shaking her head to clear the image from her mind, she brought her attention to Bandares's golden trident and ankh necklaces. Smiling at the fact that he'd made no attempt to change their default design from when former Emperor and Empress, Quortez and Felisha had bestowed them upon him.

"No. I've yet to see what you've done to him or his people. Honestly, it's really hard to watch your memories. I left off where you first encountered the Mu-waiqiao, stopping right after the conglomeration of branches and vines wilted away, just shy of when they were about to smash into your voidship," she said, letting go of his arms, wondering if he still hated the Mu-waiqiao since she'd never seen him so much as bat an eye or complain over their presence on planet Adrasteia.

"If I'd never seen his memories, I'd have thought they were friends. When he was leaving, they made the saddest colors I've ever seen come from them."

"I see, I see…but weren't you curious about what had happened to those vile, disgusting beings in that very moment? I assure you, even I'm still surprised," Bandares said.

She nodded her head ever so slightly realising he'd probably stopped caring about the Mu-waiqiao a long time ago. Most likely way before she was even born, and that his mouth was only saying those words because they were pre-programed into him.

"I'm still curious, but I'd rather come see you in person than watch your memories," she said unable to keep her mind from searching the historic records to find out when Wa'raydon had gained the alias 'Reaper of the Void'.

"Like I said before. That's because you haven't gotten far enough in my memories," he said, swallowing hard before turning towards the Emperor and nodding his head.

"Hey? What'd you do? You already challenged him, didn't you? Why? There's still a few days left to figure something out!" She screamed as the Emperor stood up in a manner that reminded her of a person who hates having to do anything.

"Takumbo, I wish you and your child the best," Emperor Dimitrius said, laying a hand on Bandares's shoulder while reaching out and touching her lower stomach.

The sensation and power his hand gave off instantly gave her powerful orgasm. Gasping for breath, trying to calm the sensations of pure, unrefined pleasure coursing through her body, she reached out and grabbed the Emperor's arm as he was turning to walk out into the arena.

"Emperor please, I'm begging you. Please stop this if you can. Show them who you are. I can feel your true power, it's so potent it has its own texture as it leaves your body and travels throughout the seven plains of existence. People don't understand what they're truly feeling from you because they can't see past your outwards nonchalant demeanor, but you can show them in a way they can understand. They just need to see a proper reference to gauge your power and ability.

Just killing them makes them angrier and want to try harder, because they think you're tricking them with help of some kind. With their mindset like this, thousands more will challenge you in the seven remaining days. Please, I'm begging you to stop this," she gasped as she took in deep gulps of air which did nothing to help clear the effect of his touch.

Returning her gaze to Bandares, she could see his face had returned to its normal scowl.

"I can't, for now I'm unfortunately stuck on this course. Humm, I see Bandares gave you his memories. With my touch, I've also given you mine. And I'm sor-...well actually... I'm not sorry. I will not allow you to stay and watch this. Oh and right now, I'm sending you on a very important mission, so make your Emperor proud okay?" Emperor Dimitrius said in a jesting, yet condescending tone, all the while producing the brightest, most blatantly fake smile she'd ever seen in her life.

"I can't stop my legs from trembling. Who? No, what kind of human being is this?" She thought, nodding her head in acceptance to his word.

"Good then," the Emperor said softly, clapping Bandares on the back as he turned and stepped into the arena, which instantly ignited many of the spectators on the far side into a booing frenzy.

Bandares's scowl changed before her eyes, lighting up into a warm, genuine smile.

"I didn't plan my life to be like this, but I made one bad decision after another. Always choosing the darkest path in life, I inadvertently carved it so deep, my son couldn't find any others to choose from. If I had any respect for her at all or if I really truly loved her at all, the least I could've done was ensure his survival, at least until he had a child or a few children of his own. That way, if he went on to the next life, there'd at least still be a part of her in this plain of existence," Bandares said in the warmest tone she'd ever heard him use, before he came and kissed her stomach.

Moving his head back, he locked eyes with her and raised his lips for a kiss.

"I understand," she whispered, kissing him softly on the lips as she mentally enquired to women all throughout the World-Ship to see if any had been willing to keep Nairn's seed after laying with him, hoping at least one felt duty bound enough to keep his mother's bloodline alive.

As she continued to enquire, Bandares pressed his forehead to hers, then turned and stepped out into the arena. In that very same moment, a brilliant burst of energy brighter than the white dwarf of the Yin't and Yin'n system unleashed, smashing into every portion of the shield surrounding the arena.

"Who'd that come from?" she wondered in both awe and horror as her escort team covered her body with their own.

A fraction of a second later, everyone's internal nano-material along with the nano-material of the World-Ship engulfed them in a tight sphere. Before the second was complete, they were launched out into the void.

"Not a soul answered me in regards to keeping Nairn's seed," she reflected solemnly as the sphere smoothly plunged into a passing 'Versus ship', in which her internal nano-cells indicated held a crew of nearly four million.

Before the sphere her and her escorts were held within even had a chance to integrate with the 'Versus Ship', it had opened up and gone through eleven one time use entanglement points, which were all to solar systems so far away from Adrasteia binary or any system even remotely familiar to her. Takumbo knew right away, whatever her mission entailed, meant she'd never see home again.

.

Solar Systems

Rock & crystal world size comparisons with Earth are based on planet surface area

Adrasteia Binary

(Inescapable)

Suns

Blue Giant: **Sekhmet**
Red Giant: **Rati**

Normal orbit is approximately four and a half light days apart

Planet 1)   Rock: **Kemet Spodos**
             Four times larger than Earth

Planet 2)   Rock: **Ta'ab**
             Eight times larger than Earth

Planet 3)   Rock: **Ta'ab Shui**
             Fourteen times larger than Earth

Planet 4)   Rock: **Cex**
             Six times larger than Earth

Planet 5)   Rock: **Vayu**
             Ten times larger than Earth

Planet 6)   Rock: **Adrasteia**
             Twelve times larger than Earth

Planet 7)   Class III, Gas Giant: **Tepeu**
             Fourteen moon-worlds orbit Gas Giant Tepeu

Planet 8)   Class II, Gas Giant: **Thoth**
             Twenty-five moon-worlds orbit Gas Giant Thoth

Planet 9)   Class I, Gas Giant: **Tezcatlipoca**
             Nine moon-worlds orbit Gas Giant Tezcatlipoca

➤ **Moon-worlds:** All forty-eight moon-worlds are at a minimum eight times larger than Earth.
➤ **Solar system population:** Two point nine trillion.

➢ **Resources:** In Adrasteia binary, only planet Adrasteia is known to have an abundance of organic based helix-materials comprising of both metal and crystal. So far, only trace amounts of helix-material have been found on all the other worlds in Adrasteia binary.

➢ **Location:** Adrasteia binary is approximately twelve Earth light years away from Heka trinary and twenty-four from Kampana trinary.

Heka Trinary

(Magic)

Suns

Blue Giant: **Shiva**
Orange Giant: **Devi**
Red Giant: **Isis**

Normal orbit is approximately four light days apart

Planet 1)	Class II, Gas Giant: **Bes**
	Fourteen moon-worlds orbit Gas Giant Bes
Planet 2)	Class II, Gas Giant: **T'ros**
	Eight moon-worlds orbit Gas Giant T'ros
Planet 3)	Class II, Gas Giant: **Bastet**
	Twenty-one moon-worlds orbit Gas Giant Bastet
Planet 4)	Class II, Gas Giant: **Seshat**
	Three moon-worlds orbit Gas Giant Seshat

➢ **Moon-worlds:** All forty-six moon-worlds are at a minimum twelve times larger than Earth.

➢ **Solar system population:** Approximately four trillion.

➢ **Resources:** The metals that comprise the moon-worlds of Heka trinary are all organic based helical structures.

➢ **Location:** Heka trinary is twelve Earth light years from Adrasteia binary and twelve from Kampana trinary.

Kampana Trinary

(Vibration)

<u>Suns</u>

Red Giant: **Swara**
Blue Giant: **Solfege**
Red Giant: **Sargam Lun-Hui**

Normal orbit is approximately seven light days apart

Planet 1)   Crystal: **Shadja**
            Eight times larger than Earth

Planet 2)   Crystal: **Rishabha**
            Eight times larger than Earth

Planet 3)   Crystal: **Kampana**
            Eight times larger than Earth

Planet 4)   Crystal: **Gandhaara**
            Ten times larger than Earth

Planet 5)   Crystal: **Madhyama**
            Twelve times larger than Earth

Planet 6)   Crystal: **Panchama**
            Fourteen times larger than Earth

Planet 7)   Crystal: **Dhaivata**
            Sixteen times larger than Earth

Planet 8)   Crystal: **Nishadam**
            The roving planet - size unknown

- ➢ **Solar system population:** Approximately one trillion.
- ➢ **Resources:** The crystals that comprise the planets of Kampana trinary are all organic based helical structures.
- ➢ **Location:** Kampana trinary is twelve Earth light years from Heka trinary and twenty-four from Adrasteia binary.

R'yu Trinary

(Primal instincts)

Suns

Red dwarf: **Kong-pa**
Red dwarf: **Ghadab**
Red dwarf: **Kama Vaasanaa**

Normal orbit is approximately one light hour apart from each other

Planet 1)   Rock: **Enyo**
                       Three times larger than Earth

Planet 2)   Rock: **R'yu**
                       Six times larger than Earth

Planet 3)   Rock: **Ekchuah**
                       Nine times larger than Earth

4th orbit ring: Broken Rock Planetoid:
                       Kali's heart
                       Estimated to have been fifteen times larger than Earth

Debris trails that comprise of Kali's heart

Hisan, Tarrapank, Vasanistirio, Umutsuzluk

5th orbit ring: Shattered planet debris trail:
                       Kali's blood
                       Estimated to have been twenty times larger than Earth

Debris trails that comprise of Kali's blood

Bnahyut, Guven, Skopos, Pengampunan

Planet 4)   Class I, Gas Giant: **Minerva**

Planet 5)   Ice Giant: **Nacon**

- ➤ **Solar system population:** Approximately one point eight trillion.
- ➤ **Location:** Sixty light years from Adrasteia binary.

163

Yin't & Yin'n Binary

(Divinity of women)

Suns

White dwarf: **Kali**
Ignited brown dwarf: **Vajrayogini**

Normal orbit is approximately eight light days apart

Planet 1)	Class V, Gas Giant: **Nigredo**
Planet 2)	Rock: **Pele** Fifty-five times larger than Earth
Planet 3)	Class IV, Gas Giant: **Oya**
Planet 4)	Class II, Gas Giant: **Dissolutio**
Planet 5)	Class II, Gas Giant: **Separationem**
Planet 6)	Rock: **Mahavairocana** Three times larger than Earth
Planet 7)	Class II, Gas Giant: **Albedo**
Planet 8)	Ice Giant: **Conjunctio**
Planet 9)	Rock: **Fermentationem** Thirteen times larger than Earth
Planet 10)	Rock: **Marici** Eight times larger than Earth
Planet 11)	Ice Giant: **Citrinitas**
Planet 12)	Class I, Gas Giant: **Rubedo**
Planet 13)	Rock: **Tattvasamgraha** Five times larger than Earth
Planet 14)	Ice Giant: **Inhib**
Planet 15)	Rock: **Yin't** Thirty-four times larger than Earth

Planet 16)   Rock: **Yin'n**
            Twenty-one times larger than Earth

➢ **Orbit path:** Yin't and Yin'n are tidally locked together and travel throughout the entire binary system in a Horseshoe Orbit.

➢ **Solar system population:** Approximately four point two trillion.

➢ **Location:** Eighty-six light years from Adrasteia binary.

Globular cluster Tyche
Four moon sector

(Apsaras of the final hope)

Sun

Blue Hyper giant: **Kamakhya**

Y Dwarf Hyang's normal orbit is approximately twenty-one light hours away from Kamakhya

Planet 1)   Y Dwarf: **Hyang**

Moons Orbiting Y Dwarf Hyang

Moon 1)   **Aanjay**
Three hundred seventy-seven times larger than Earth

Moon 2)   **Utari**
Two hundred thirty-three times larger than Earth

Moon 3)   **Nur**
One hundred forty-four times larger than Earth

Moon 4)   **Ningrum**
Eighty-nine times larger than Earth

➢ **Globular cluster population:** Approximately two billion. Note that this population count is only based on Adrasteia Empire's current presence since Adrasteians only go to the four moon sector for special occasions.

➢ **Location:** Thirty-six light years from Adrasteia binary.